# Taste of Wrath

# ALSO BY MATT WALLACE

# TASTE OF
# WRATH

## MATT WALLACE

A TOM DOHERTY ASSOCIATES BOOK
NEW YORK

This is a work of fiction. All of the characters, organizations, and
events portrayed in this novella are either products of the author's
imagination or are used fictitiously.

TASTE OF WRATH

Copyright © 2018 by Matt Wallace

Cover design by Peter Lutjen
Cover photographs © Getty Images

Edited by Lee Harris

A Tor.com Book
Published by Tom Doherty Associates
175 Fifth Avenue
New York, NY 10010

www.tor.com

Tor® is a registered trademark of
Macmillan Publishing Group, LLC.

ISBN 978-0-7653-9324-1 (ebook)
ISBN 978-0-7653-9325-8 (trade paperback)

First Edition: April 2018

*For Mitch*

PART I

# WAR IN THREE COURSES: IN THE SOUP

# MEET THE NEW BOSS, SAME AS THE OLD BOSS

Getting Jett Hollinshead down is no easy feat. Her enthusiasm usually has to be measured with the same technology that ranks things like tornados, hurricanes, and the toxicity of *Rick and Morty* fandom. Standing in Bronko's office, however, she doesn't just look downtrodden at the moment; she looks defeated. Jett watches Bronko as he sits behind his desk, filling out purchase orders by hand, a sight that usually calms and reassures her everything is proceeding normally, but today she knows that isn't true, perhaps never will be again.

"What is it, Jett?" the executive chef finally asks her. "Did Chanel stop makin' suits or something?"

"I wish that was my only issue at the moment," she grumbles.

Bronko grunts. "This *must* be serious, then. You fittin' to tell me, or are you just planning to stand there and wring your hands all afternoon?"

Jett practically comes apart at the joints. "Oh, Byron, it's a catastrophe! All our events have been cancelled! *All* of them!"

Bronko's hand finally stops moving. He sighs as if the weight of a large planet has just settled upon his shoulders. Placing his pen atop his decades-old blotter, he reclines against the towering winged back of his throne-like leather chair and regards Jett with a wearied, joyless smile.

"Well, now, that's not altogether unexpected, is it?"

"It's worse than that, Byron; all of our vendors, all of my venue contacts, they're all either walking away from us or no longer returning my calls, texts, or emails. I can't access our corporate accounts. They've all been frozen. Sin du Jour has effectively been rendered off-line."

Bronko nods. "Then we may have ourselves much bigger problems a-comin', don't you think?"

"You think this presages an attack?" Jett asks him.

"I think whatever's comin' has been comin' for a goodly while and we're finally running outta road."

"Then . . . is staying here the right thing, Byron? I . . . I would never consider *abandoning* you or the staff—"

"O' course you wouldn't, Jett. You're tougher than a bullwhacker's steak dinner. I know that."

She seems to take genuine solace in those words, nodding along with them. "Thank you. It's just that . . ."

"Should we *all* run, is what you're puttin' out there."

"Yes."

"Jett, darlin', there ain't no runnin' from this. There's nowhere in this world any one of us *could* hide, maybe not even in any other world. We've done all we can to fortify this place in our favor. This is the best any of us is gonna do."

"Then is it time to call everyone in? What's the word? 'Bunker' and wait for whatever's coming?"

"It may be time to give everyone the choice, or at least let 'em know where we're at."

Jett nods, resolutely, forcing the steel calm over her she's spent her entire life cultivating.

"I'll take care of it, Byron."

"You're a blessin', my dear."

She offers him the most genuine smile she can manage. Jett turns toward the door and immediately stops, nearly leaping from her heels and letting out a yelp.

"You startled the bejesus out of me! Will you kindly announce yourself before just . . . poofing like that?"

"Apologies, ma'am," a nasal, dreary voice answers Jett.

Bronko leans over the padded arm of his chair and peers around Jett's lithe figure. The squat, ink-animated form of Droopy Hound is standing in Bronko's office, staring through them both into some unimpressive oblivion only the living cartoon character can see with its dour eyes. Droopy Hound has clad himself in a plain blue guard's uniform, no doubt a mockery of his current station in life. A demon inserted into Sin du Jour by Allensworth as the building's magical security system, Marcus mystically reprogrammed the malevolent spirit to answer only to Bronko and the staff.

"What do you want?" Bronko bluntly asks the apparition.

"You have a visitor, sir," he informs Bronko. "He's waiting in the lobby. I've taken the liberty of magically isolating the entrances and exits available to him as a precaution."

"Who is he?"

Droopy Hound shrugs his perpetually sagging shoulders. "I can only tell you he's human, sir."

Bronko sighs, heavily. "Fine, then."

"Thank you for your service, Mr. . . . Hound," Jett offers, diplomatically.

"A deal is a deal, ma'am," the toon replies simply before evaporating with a static-filled dissolve.

"Well, at least our efforts to secure Sin du Jour seem to be working," Jett says.

Bronko stands, grunting as the bones in both of his knees audibly pop.

"I ever tell you about my first joint, the one I opened myself, without backers or venture capitalists and the like?"

Jett shakes her head.

"Li'l roadhouse joint about twenty miles from the border in South Texas." Bronko opens the top right-hand drawer of his desk. "It was a rough crowd, and I mean the staff, not the customers. I hadta take what I could get, for the most part. I wouldn't be surprised if there were more outstanding warrants in that kitchen than high school diplomas."

"I can imagine."

"So, I learned the hard way, whenever you had to fire a body from an employee pool like that, you best stick a paring knife in your apron just in case they took to the news poorly."

Jett's eyes narrow in confusion. "I . . . That's a quaint anecdote, Byron, but why that? Why now?"

Bronko reaches inside the drawer. The knife he removes from it isn't meant for peeling fruits and vegetables; it's a hunting blade with a wicked clip point and a handle fashioned from elk bone. He reaches behind his wide body and carefully tucks the blade through his belt at the small of his back, draping the hem of his chef's smock over it to conceal it from sight.

"No idea," he says with a grin.

Jett shakes her head. "Byron . . ."

"Let's go greet our guest. Hell, maybe somebody here won the damn lottery; wouldn't that be a thing?"

Jett can't help smiling, and this time it's strong and clear and mirthful.

The two of them exit Bronko's office and walk the winding corridors toward the front of the ancient brick building. There's no visible barrier between the corridor and the lobby, but as Bronko and Jett pass through the archway, they can both feel the electric edge of magic raising the tiny hairs on their exposed flesh.

The man waiting for them defines nondescript. Despite being the lobby's only occupant, it's easy to look right past him, almost as if he's a background actor in a scene from a movie, placed there to be ignored. He's perhaps thirty-five, wearing a plain gray suit and tie and carrying a tan valise. His expression is passive but pleasant enough.

"Can I help you?" Bronko asks him.

"Good afternoon to you, Chef Luck, Miss Hollinshead," the man they have definitely never met before greets them amiably. "I'm Sin du Jour's new liaison. My name is Allensworth."

# GOODWILL

"You're too old and too slow to take me. Also—and this is unrelated—I'm better-looking than you and always have been."

Ritter ignores the giggles Marcus's comments elicit from the children, but his younger brother feeds on the reaction. The two men circle each other atop the interlocking foam mats assembled beneath their bare feet, both of them wearing martial arts gis. Ritter moves slowly and deliberately, stalking Marcus like a predator with his fists balled at his waist, while Marcus bounces jubilantly on his feet, hands raised and fingers practically twitching.

Beyond the mats, an assemblage of thirty children, ranging in age from five to twelve, watch them attentively. They're all regular faces around the makeshift recreational center Hara established in a converted warehouse in Bed-Stuy for the neighborhood kids. Since Hara's funeral, Ritter has spent as much time here as he can to ensure the place stays open.

The kids aren't Ritter and Marcus's only spectators.

Cindy is sitting on an empty milk crate off to the side, hunched over her fatigues-clad knees, hiding a steady grin in a Styrofoam cup filled with coffee.

"You see, kids," Ritter says to the children without shifting his focus from Marcus, "all bullies are talkers. They *love* to talk. They do it for a couple of reasons. One reason is to pump themselves up, to hide the fear they all feel. The other reason they talk is to distract you and intimidate you, get you to doubt yourself. The best thing to do is ignore their words. There's no place for words in a fight. It's their body doing the only talking you want to listen to, the way they move their feet, their shoulders, even their eyes."

"I'm just telling truths over here," Marcus claims, then lunges at his brother.

Ritter slaps away a series of front kicks, and then ducks a flawlessly executed spinning heel kick that sails harmlessly overhead. Marcus tries to recover from the missed strike by immediately leaping forward and driving the heel of his palm into Ritter's face, but Ritter quickly slaps his wrist off-course before delivering the back of the same hand into the side of Marcus's head. It isn't a particularly painful blow, but it is delivered with enough force to knock him off-balance.

Marcus quickly turns away from Ritter and walks across the mat. There's a grin on his face, but it's clear he's at least a little embarrassed by the quick exchange and its results.

"*Older and slower* are different than *old and slow*," Ritter says to him.

Marcus nods. "Uh-huh. Hey, have you taught them about the element of surprise yet?"

With that, Marcus lets out a sudden and loud battle cry as he rushes forward, dropping his head and attempting to spear Ritter to the mat like an NFL player. Ritter leans forward and spreads his legs, digging his heels into the mat as Marcus barrels into him just above the waist. The leverage prevents Marcus from taking Ritter down and allows Ritter to encircle Marcus's torso with his arms. Heaving his brother's feet into the air, Ritter flips him over and drops him onto the mat.

Marcus lands hard on his back, oxygen fleeing through his mouth and nostrils like an angry stampede. A wave of *ooh*s and *ah*s passes over the children watching.

Cindy, on the other hand, laughs into her cup.

"You see what just happened, kids?" Ritter asks them, ignoring his distressed sibling. "Marcus wanted to win. He wanted to beat me. That's what he was trying to do. That's all he cared about. I was just trying to survive. I wasn't thinking about winning. And I never went after him. I let him come to me and I countered his attacks. That's what self-defense is."

Meanwhile, Marcus has turned over and crawled to the far edge of the mat in front of Cindy, slowly taking air back into his lungs.

She sips her coffee and looks down at him with a grin. "Well, that was some sad-ass shit to watch."

"Pretty sexy, huh?" he asks with a grin, looking up at her from the mat cattishly.

Cindy shakes her head. "And I just bet more empty-headed bitches have fallen for that fake-ass Han Solo ish than have turned it down."

"It's working on you, just slowly."

"You ain't there yet, boy."

Marcus drops his head in mock defeat, but when he lifts it again, he's only grinning wider.

"Did I hear 'yet'?" he asks. "Did I?"

Cindy offers no further comment.

There's a knock on the front gate, the metal sheet ringing long after the pounding stops.

"All right," Ritter addresses the kids. "Shoes off, on the mat, and we'll do some sparring drills, okay? Get yourselves set up and pick a partner."

He walks off the mat and over to the front entrance. When Ritter pulls the heavy aluminum door aside, no one is waiting for him beyond it. All he finds is a metal shopping cart loaded down with electronic equipment. He sifts through it briefly, looking for a note or some other documentation, finding none. He examines the alley outside the warehouse, but there isn't a single soul in sight.

"What's all that?" Cindy asks as Ritter wheels the shopping cart inside.

He shrugs. "Anonymous donation would be my best guess."

"Dude, that's all really high-end shit."

Cindy smacks him on the arm. "What did I just say about watching your mouth and being among little people, boy?"

"I'm just saying, this is all the latest gaming gear. Every console on the market, looks like. And all this audio equipment is top-shelf."

"Wait," Cindy says, her expression darkening. "This is Moon's. All this crap belongs to him. I recognize it from his garbage masher of an apartment."

"I thought he preferred video games to human sexual contact," Ritter muses.

Cindy shakes her head. "Sad little turd thinks he can buy us with some secondhand PlayStations."

"That's not a bad price," Marcus comments. "Even aftermarket, this stuff is worth—"

"I don't give a single damn!" Cindy insists. "He lied to us. Hara got fragged because he lied to us. You don't screw your team like that. Boy never gave a damn about being part of this thing."

"It's a very un-Moon-like gesture," Ritter points out.

Cindy stares at him, incredulous. "Don't tell me you fallin' for this shit."

"I'm just stating a fact," Ritter says with his usual stony neutrality.

"Is that PlayStation 4?" one of the kids shouts from across the warehouse. "*And* Xbox One?"

In the next moment, there are fifty kids clamoring over the new video gaming equipment as if a celebrity has stopped by the warehouse.

"I guess we're hooking this stuff up?" Marcus asks them both.

"Dammit, Moon," Cindy mutters to herself.

Ritter says no more, but as they begin unloading the shopping cart and untangling the jungle of wires accompanying the many electronic pieces, there is an undeniable grin tugging at the right corner of his mouth.

# *RESTRUCTURING* IS ANOTHER WORD FOR *COLLAPSE*

"You're not Allensworth," Bronko says. "If'n he was going to change his face, I imagine he'd go with something more ostentatious-like."

"Byron!" Jett chastises him.

"That's quite all right, Miss Hollinshead," the man who introduced himself as Allensworth assures her. "I've been apprised of your jovial personality, Chef Luck, and I'm sure I'll come to enjoy it immensely."

"When's the part where you explain why you have the same name—"

"Think of the name as an operational title, if it helps you," their self-proclaimed new liaison offers. "I am replacing the man you knew as Allensworth in the role he filled."

"So . . . what happened to the previous owner of your operational title?" Bronko asks, summoning his best acting chops, playing the role of man who didn't watch the former Allensworth take an eight-inch chef's knife through his kidney.

"That's still being determined," the new Allensworth says. "I'm afraid my predecessor's behavior had become rather erratic as of late. Obviously, oversight in our department always does prove ... challenging.... However, I fear his autonomy got the best of him. You needn't concern yourselves with the matter any further. As I said, I'll be taking up his duties henceforth."

Bronko and Jett exchange a quick, tight glance, the kind of thing conspirators probably shouldn't do.

If their new Allensworth takes note, it's a deeply internal process.

"Well, then ... good to know you, Allensworth," Bronko says.

The nondescript man smiles without his eyes joining in on the expression. "Likewise, Chef."

"Excuse me," Jett interjects. "Can you tell us why our corporate accounts have been frozen and all of our upcoming events have been cancelled?"

"It's standard procedure, Miss Hollinshead. All of the projects overseen by my predecessor are now under review. That includes this edifice and its operations. Those operations have to be suspended during that period of review. We apologize for any inconvenience this causes. I assure you it will be a noninvasive and hopefully brief inconvenience before everything returns to its usual day-to-day."

"Some advance warnin' would've been nice," Bronko tells him.

"Byron, don't pester the poor man," Jett says, but her eyes are warning Bronko not to press their luck. "He's obviously under a lot of pressure. Taking on a new high-level position is never easy."

"That's quite all right, Miss Hollinshead. Again, I apologize for the disruption. We are attempting to right the ship, as it were, as soon as possible. In the interim, I'd advise you all to return to your homes and wait for things to settle. As soon as we've performed our due diligence, you will hopefully be able to return to work."

"So, y'all have no clue where Allensworth is?" Bronko asks. "The other one, I mean. The last one, or however you want to call it."

"As I said, you needn't trouble yourself with any matters involving my predecessor. It's being handled."

"All right, then."

The new Allensworth offers them another joyless smile. "All right, then. It's a pleasure finally meeting both of you. I hope you'll enjoy your impromptu time off. I promise I'll be in touch."

"It was a pleasure meeting you too, Mr. Allensworth," Jett says, slipping into her best professional demeanor.

"Charmed," Bronko adds stiffly.

They watch Allensworth leave, neither Bronko nor Jett

moving or even so much as breathing audibly for almost a full thirty seconds after the doors close behind their new liaison.

"How can they *not* know?" Jett whispers frantically. "How can they not know what happened at Gluttony Bay?"

"Allensworth, the *real* one, must've gone rogue even bigger'n we suspected," Bronko whispers back. "Maybe his people never even knew he was involved with Gluttony Bay. Lord knows what else those people do with their time, what else they oversee. They trusted Allensworth to handle things with the Sceadu. Or at least they did."

"So . . . are we . . . are we in the clear, Byron? Is it over?"

Bronko shakes his head, no relief whatsoever revealed in his expression. In fact, his brow seemed weighted more heavily than before.

"No," he says. "I'm worried it's worse, actually. Allensworth is totally off the reservation now."

"But he's gone, isn't he? I thought—"

"I don't believe Allensworth is dead."

"Which Allensworth?"

"Jett, c'mon, girl."

"Right, right. But you said Lena stabbed Allensworth!"

"She did."

"And you said that awful restaurant prison place blew up!"

"It did."

"Then how can he be alive?"

"You don't plan to overthrow the whole damn world without settin' up contingencies, Jett. Y'all didn't know that Allensworth like I did. Trust me. He's capable of things you can't even think of. He's still out there, and I doubt his plans have changed any. And if he was pissed at us before, he's murderous now."

"Then shouldn't we tell the new Allensworth? Ask for his help? We can't face something like this alone!"

"How can we trust him any more than the last one? Besides, if they find out about Gluttony Bay or that Vargas is still with us, who's to say they won't lump us in with the old Allensworth? Just to be safe?"

"Then what *are* we going to do, Byron?"

"What we were doing already," Bronko says with a hard edge of resolve in his voice. "We're going to get ready. And we're going to reach out to anyone we *can* afford to trust. Because you're right: we can't do this all on our own."

Jett takes a deep, cleansing breath. "Very well. Who *do* we trust? To whom can we reach out?"

"To my mind?" Bronko muses. "Satisfied customers are worth a shot."

# MAKEUP CLASSES

Ryland Phelan only has one picture of his father. It's a Polaroid, taken in the early 1990s, its upper right-hand corner partially melted into a multicolored oil slick. His father was in his forties at the time. He looked a lot like Ryland, except sober and well kempt. In the Polaroid, the man appears to be pouring water from a drinking glass into a wineglass half-filled with cheap red. That's all the layperson would observe, probably barely taking note of the changing medallion hanging from a thick chain around his neck.

Growing up, Ryland hated alchemy. He watched his father eke out a meager living performing genuine miracles from which he was forbidden by some unknowable force from directly profiting. He could turn lead into gold as long as he did it for someone else, but if his father tried to spend that gold, he'd find himself holding worthless metal again. Ryland watched his dissatisfied mother run off with some Welsh warlock prick who wasn't bound by a bullshit ethereal half-morality, half-karma net.

Ryland learned to think of alchemy as peasant magic,

only good for serving the nobility. He had to be forced to learn the trade by his old man, the way some children are made to work in their parent's shop to learn responsibility. The real problem, he later discovered, was that Ryland is a natural alchemist. Worsening that dilemma, he wasn't good at much else. The older he got, the more Ryland resented that alchemy was his only true talent. The more resentful he grew, the more he drank, until he couldn't remember which one filled him with that constant sense of self-loathing.

He pondered that very question as he lay on the filthy, cluttered floor of his antiquated recreational vehicle, clutching a half-empty bottle of wine in one hand and the Polaroid of his father in the other.

"You were a silly sod," he says to the man in the photograph. "You were that. Why could you not have taught yourself pyromancy or some such shite? We could have spent the money from an insurance fire."

A knock at his RV's door breaks Ryland free of his drunken reveries, although it does nothing for the condition of the battered space between his temples.

"Please desist immediately!" he yells at the door. "Have you no sense of decency?"

Ryland stuffs the Polaroid into his pants pocket and drains the bottle of wine in a single prolonged swig. What feels like an eternity later, he manages to lumber to the door. Practically ripping it from its cheap hinges, he finds Moon awaiting him at the foot of the RV steps.

"What's changed about you?" Ryland asks him. "Were you Asian before?"

"What? No."

"Is that somehow an offensive question?"

"I . . . don't know, actually. I just cleaned up a little, that's all."

"Ah, yes, I see it now."

Moon has actually shaved his jaw and neck smooth and combed his hair. New jeans and a clean T-shirt referencing pop culture have replaced his customary uniform of ragged pop culture–referencing T-shirt and distressed jeans.

"Have you come here strictly to flaunt your new aesthetic?" Ryland asks.

"No, I need to talk to you."

"Very well. Come inside, have a drink or perhaps several dozen in rapid succession."

"I'll come in, but I'm not drinking anymore."

"Fine, fine. We'll have herbal refreshments, then."

"I'm off the weed, too."

Ryland squints at him, trying to scrutinize Moon through the drunken fog.

"You're behaving suspiciously akin to an individual preparing to espouse some sort of newfound yet somehow deeply held religious philosophy."

"It's not like that, I swear."

Ryland makes a dissatisfied sound that might have been an attempt at actual words, and steps aside to allow Moon entry into the RV.

"What's on your mind, then?" Ryland asks, collapsing into the one seat in the space that isn't hosting an array of litter.

Moon brushes off enough counter space in the kitchenette to lean against.

"Look, I had fun hanging out with you, drinking, smoking weed, fucking off, playing video games. But I should've been doing what Bronko told me to do, for my team. You were supposed to teach me this alchemy stuff."

"Which we both concurred was an absurd notion on its absurd little face."

"Yeah, well, then I should've told Bronko no, but I didn't. I said I'd do something and I need to do it."

Ryland fishes a crumpled packet of cigarettes and a scuffed Bic lighter from his breast pocket. He pulls a stick from the packet with his teeth and lights it, taking a long drag.

"Weren't you fired from this establishment?" he asks in the smoky wake of exhaling.

"Not exactly, no."

"Oh. Well, that is a shame, that. I was going to congratulate you."

Moon sighs, exasperated. "Dude, listen, I want you to teach me. I mean, really teach me, for real."

Ryland stares up at him as if Moon has slipped into conversational Sanskrit.

"Come again?"

"Teach me to be an alchemist," Moon repeats, slowly.

Ryland takes another long, deep drag and fills the cramped, stinking space with acrid smoke.

"That is a truly hideous notion," he concludes.

"I need to learn. I could've helped my team if I'd learned. I could've . . . I could've saved . . . I just need to do it for real, that's all. Look, I'm not gonna lay some bullshit on you like you owe me or anything, 'cuz you don't, but I really need you to do this."

"You're asking me to relive boyhood trauma, my young friend. The instruction of alchemy is quite possibly my worst memory, save losing my virginity—a tale I'll benevolently spare you."

"What else have you got to do, dude?"

"That is hardly a reason, let alone reason enough."

"I'll buy all your booze the whole time, the good stuff, *and* I'll hook you up with my weed guy. He's Jamaican. I'm just sayin.'"

Ryland's expression changes, becoming more quizzical than confused or irritated as he looks up at Moon.

"This is a thing you really want, isn't it?"

"I *need* it," Moon insists.

"Huh. I wish my father were still alive. I'd introduce you. He spent his whole life wishing my mother had given birth to a willing pupil for him."

Ryland digs the Polaroid out of his pocket and rests it in his lap, staring down at the image of the old man.

Moon is silent, allowing Ryland his moment of reflection.

"Well," he concludes, "I suppose if you'll see me functionally impaired for the duration, I can impart a few lessons."

Moon's eyes widen. "Seriously?"

Ryland shrugs. "It'll be a change of pace, at least."

"Great. That's great, man. Thank you. Where do we start?"

Ryland holds up the Polaroid of his father, squinting at it in the stray beams of light that have found a way through the dirty streaks on the RV's windows.

"I suppose we'll begin with water into wine," he says.

# SAFE HOUSE

Halfway up the stairs of the old building in Williamsburg, Bronko freezes as a sudden and penetrating dread fills his mind and infects the rest of his body.

"It's all right," Ritter assures him. "It's a defensive enchantment, to keep people away. It's not real."

Bronko digs a hand into his breast over his now-pounding heart. "It damn well feels real."

"It's not. Think of something peaceful, something that makes you feel calm. It helps."

His breathing has become staccato. "I never . . . been inside this building before. I always . . . leave their packages on the fire escape."

"Think calming thoughts, boss," Ritter bids him.

"Right."

They hike the remaining steps, Ritter slowing his pace to remain close to Bronko for support. It's slow going the rest of the way, but he makes it.

They hear a hollow plastic thunk repeating over and over as they round the corner. A little redheaded girl, perhaps six, is standing in the middle of the hallway, bouncing one of those big rubber balls they keep in perilous caged bins at big box stores. When she spots Ritter and Bronko, the girl freezes right after tossing the ball back at the floor. When it bounces up in front of her chest, her hands don't grab it, yet the ball never returns to the floor. It remains there, hovering perfectly still in the space between her tiny, inert hands.

"I guess we're on the right floor," Bronko says quietly.

The little redheaded girl turns and runs away, pumping her little arms and legs as fast as she can will them to move. She beats feet for a red door several yards down the hall, sliding to a stop there and pounding on its surface until the door opens just wide enough to allow her small body to slip through. It closes quickly after her.

The rubber ball finally bounces against the floor.

"Is that the one?" Ritter asks.

"It's hard to tell from the outside which window goes where," Bronko says.

Every light in the hallway begins flickering. In the next moment, they begin blinking off until the entire length of the hallway is cast into pitch-darkness. It doesn't make any sense; it's midday and there's a window at the end of the hall. Sunlight should illuminate most of the corridor, yet not a single sunray seems to penetrate the abject darkness that's enveloped them.

"What was that mule shit about calming thoughts?"

Bronko asks Ritter, who he can no longer see.

"Just stay where you are and wait," Ritter instructs him.

"Don't you have some magical doodad to deal with this like you always do?"

"I didn't bring anything like that."

"Why the hell not?"

"I didn't come here for a fight," Ritter says stonily.

The lights return in a single flash. When they do, Bronko is aware the hallway has changed without immediately seizing upon why or how. A moment later, he realizes all of the doors are now gone. The walls on both sides of them are smooth and unbroken all the way down the length of the corridor.

A tall woman with the longest hair either of them has ever seen is standing in the hallway several yards in front of Bronko and Ritter. Her mass of blond tendrils falls far past her waist, each one curling like a spring. The lines in her face speak far more of experience than age. The same is true for the weight of her gaze. She wears a simple summer dress with a pattern of bird silhouettes in flight, and leather sandals that look like something from a Roman drama.

"How do, Cassie?" Bronko greets her, trying to think of those calming things like Ritter advised.

"You're not supposed to come here like this, Chef

Luck," she says in a deep, mellifluous voice. "While we greatly appreciate your aid, if there is a problem with our deliveries, you were given a number to call. Showing up like this endangers all of us."

"I understand, and I do apologize, but what I have to say has to be said in person. Plus, I have an introduction to make. Ritter, this is Cassandra. She runs the place, if you couldn't tell."

Cassandra looks at Ritter for the first time, seeming to gaze above him more than at him. "Your aura is . . ."

As her voice trails off, Cassandra's eyes widen and fill with storm clouds. "I know what you are," she says.

"Pardon, ma'am?" Bronko asks.

"You're a hunter!" she shouts accusingly. "Don't deny it!"

"I was," Ritter admits, calmly.

Cassandra's gaze darts to Bronko, his perceived betrayal written clearly in her eyes.

"Why would you bring him here?" she demands.

"He's the man floating the bill, Cassie," Bronko informs her. "Ritter set all of this up for you, all of you. He had me be the face to avoid exactly this here exchange we're having now, but he's the one put up the scratch to start this safe house, and he's been carrying you and yours every day since."

"He hunted us!" she practically shrieks at them both.

"I can see it! He wears the blood like a halo! How many did you kill? How many did you burn? How many were scarcely children?"

"Twenty-three," Ritter answers, voice barely a whisper. "Most of them looked like children to me."

His earnestness and obvious remorse catch Cassandra off guard, but her rage is barely dissipated by either.

"He was a hunter, Cass," Bronko confirms once more. "He *was*. When he figured out he was on the wrong side, he left. He's been making contrition ever since, and I don't figure he'll ever stop."

"It's not enough," she insists. "He can't buy redemption with a few sandwiches and some blankets, not for what he's done, what his *kind* have done."

"No one's here askin' for redemption, or even forgiveness. You can be as hateful as you want, you have the right, but I don't see as you'll stop being practical. How many of y'all are there livin' here now? You gonna put 'em on the street because you don't like where your rent money comes from?"

"No," Cassandra relents without hesitation. "No, I won't do that. He can assuage his guilt all he wants if it means I'm able to keep my girls safe. But he is not welcome here. Not ever. If you didn't come for forgiveness, what did you come for?"

"We need your help," Bronko says. "And maybe it's

an awful thing to ask after what y'all have been through, but if we don't survive, then this place don't survive, and that's what's on the line: survival, all of our survival. There's somethin' coming for us, and we need help, the kinda help only folks with powers like yours can give."

"Asking me, or any woman here, to help protect this man is too much, Chef. It's too much to ask at any price."

"What's coming for us," Bronko continues, "they're the same folks he used to work for, the ones who hunted you and yours. If we can stop 'em, we can maybe change things for all of you, help take y'all out of the line of fire once and for all."

Cassandra hesitates, considering the truth in his words. Her chin tilts up slightly as she regards Bronko.

Watching her, he knows she's trying to see the possible future he's just described. He can see that she wants to believe it.

In the end, however, that vision crumbles for her and she lowers her chin with a sigh.

"It's not enough," she says. "Not to help him, and not to risk our lives. We defend ourselves when attacked, but I won't ask my girls to go looking for a fight. I won't. If that means leaving this place and finding another, so be it."

Ritter steps forward. "I'll offer more," he practically begs her. "I'll offer whatever it takes to make things right and to convince you to help us. We need each other, whether you want it to be that way or not. I swear to you."

Cassandra looks at him for the second time, and for the first time, she appears to really see him and not the aura he carries with him.

"It's a price you couldn't possibly pay," she assures him darkly.

Ritter looks from the witch to Bronko. When he returns his gaze to Cassandra, the darkness in his eyes matches hers.

"Try me," he says.

# PITCH MEETING

"I thought you said we were going to the Royal Goblin Palace," Lena asks, staring up at what is clearly Mister Ramon's Artisan Unisex Hair Salon on East 76th Street.

"I said we were goin' to *a* royal goblin palace," Bronko corrects her. "And this here is it."

"It makes sense if you give it a minute," Ritter assures Lena in his typical dry way.

"Fine," she says. "Where's the door, then?"

Where the entrance should be, there's only a constant curtain of falling water.

Bronko grunts. "You're in a mood today, ain't ya?"

"Yes, Chef, I'm in a *mood*. I'm in a my-best-friend-is-being-exorcised-tonight-hopefully-before-the-guy-who-put-an-evil-assassin-spirit-inside-him-comes-back-to-kill-us-all-and-we've-been-cut-off-by-our-only-lifeline kind of mood."

"Fair 'nuff," Bronko says. "Let's see what we can't do about the last part."

The three of them walk up the ornate building's marble steps. As they approach the waterfall, blue light suddenly irradiates the constant streams. The water parts before them from the middle as if by magic.

"I already hate this place," Lena mutters.

The foyer of the salon is a clear floor covering a colorful koi pond (because *of course* it is, Lena thinks). Music that is equal parts techno and new age is being piped through speakers that seem to be embedded beneath them somehow. She can actually feel the grating noise on her legs. The simultaneously floral and septic smell of hair-treatment chemicals is more than cloying; it's like a small child's fist being rammed down her throat and up her nostrils.

Lena decides her every sense hates this place.

They wait over two spawning koi, taking in the afternoon operation of the salon. It's like watching extraordinarily beautiful people being professionally groomed in a museum where grooming is the main exhibit. Even the stylists and aestheticians look like mannequins from a Rodeo Drive clothing store come to life.

A moment later, a perfectly bronzed man whose cotton T-shirt is clinging to his chiseled abs like syrup poured into the crevasses of a waffle jogs up to them excitedly.

"Chef Luck!" he exclaims, spreading his equally chiseled arms to embrace Bronko. "Such a pleasure to have you back!"

Lena looks up at Bronko. "Back?"

"A man can't enjoy an exfoliatin' seaweed wrap now and again?" he says as he hugs the taut stylist. "How does it, Cesar?"

"I am fabulous," Cesar attests. "What can we do for you today, Chef?"

"I heard the rulin' family is in town. We need a brief audience with the King."

Cesar's plastic enthusiasm melts into something surprised and more than slightly baffled.

Bronko darkens as he sees the stylist's expression change.

"Was I misinformed?" he asks.

"No," Cesar says quickly. "No, the power is certainly here. It's just that—"

"What is it, Cesar?"

Cesar sighs, reaching out and patting Bronko's catcher's mitt of a hand with his much slighter palm.

"Wait here," he bids the trio. "I'll see what I can do."

The stylist turns and trots off before Bronko can question him further.

"Well, that was weird," Lena says, dubious.

"Maybe the King's already written us off," Ritter offers.

Lena frowns. "Or forgotten about us."

Bronko waves them both off. "He ain't like that. He remembers. This is our best play. Trust me. No one in our

Rolodex can help us more than the goblin royal family."

"What's a Rolodex?" Lena asks.

Bronko sighs, shaking his head. "I am so damn old."

Ritter reaches up and pats his shoulder reassuringly, and Bronko nods a halfhearted thanks.

"Looks like half the cast of that show based on the *Archie* comics is here getting facials and frosted tips," Lena observes, looking around the salon.

"I thought frosted tips were out," Ritter asks without a trace of irony in his voice.

Lena shrugs. "I just said a hair thing. I dunno. I've used the same brush since I was fourteen."

"That's kinda disgustin', Tarr," Bronko says.

"Yeah, well, developing a detailed beauty regimen never seemed—"

Bronko waits for the rest, but it doesn't come. He looks down at her impatiently.

"Finish your thought, Tarr."

She doesn't answer him. Lena's every facial muscle has gone completely slack.

Ritter turns his head to regard her. Both he and Bronko stare at Lena's gobsmacked face in confusion.

"Holy fucking shit," she finally blurts out.

"What is it?" Ritter asks.

Lena waves a hand in front of her disjointedly as she rambles, "It's, that's, it's . . . it's like, *all* the Chrises. It's all the Chrises in Hollywood, *all* of them, from all the movies. They're right there. Together. They're coming towards us. Every Chris. It's like a meme, only I want to have sex with it."

"Tarr, kindly recork yourself," Bronko instructs her.

"I'm sorry, Chef, I don't usually star-fuck, but *damn*, that is a lot of handsome all together—"

"Tarr!"

"Yes, Chef," she says, and then deliberately says no more.

Four living *People* magazine covers walk towards the trio in perfect unison, all of them blond save one, all of them smiling as if there's a red carpet beneath their feet, all of them clad in identical ashen-gray body-hugging cable-knit sweaters, and all of them with just the right amount of beard stubble darkening their equally granite jawlines.

————

Ritter frowns. "The Council of Chrises. I've heard about them. This isn't good, boss."

"Nope," Bronko quietly confirms, putting on his best poker face.

"Chef Luck!" the muscled Australian Chris, who stands several inches taller than the others, warmly greets

Bronko. "I haven't seen you since you catered my third twenty-ninth birthday! Those Colorado chili poppers were killer!"

"Why wasn't I invited to that?" the dark-haired Chris, the one who plays the blond-haired leader of the all-star superhero team in those movies, asks.

"You were making that indie with the train and the snow and the whatever," Australian Chris reminds him.

"Did you get a Spirit nom for that?" the Chris who used to be fat before he was cast as the leader of that *other* superhero team asks.

Dark-haired Chris shrugs. "Probably. I don't know. I do it for the love."

"You should tweet that," the Chris from the rebooted spaceship movies says, too earnestly *not* to be sarcastic.

"I asked to see the King," Bronko interrupts them, trying and failing not to sound impatient. "No offense, gentlemen. It's nice to see y'all. But is he in town, or not?"

"The King stepped down," Australian Chris informs him. "It was time for him to take a break for a few generations. You may've heard about his untimely 'death' in the news."

"Uh, yeah," Bronko confirms, trying and failing not to sound insultingly facetious. "Just once or twice."

"What can *we* do for you?" starship-captain Chris asks

pointedly, folding his cable-knit arms over his cable-knit chest.

"What the hell is happening right now?" Lena asks anyone who might be able to rationalize anything that's occurring around her.

"When the Goblin King retires from the public eye," Ritter explains, "the Council of Chrises takes interim power until a new King is confirmed."

"Meaning these four here are in charge for now," Bronko adds.

"You gentlemen know your goblin politics," formerly fat Chris commends Ritter and Bronko.

"Wait, that doesn't make *any* sense," Lena says. "How can there be a council of Chrises that takes over for the Goblin King? These guys have only been movie stars for like ten years."

"Well, that's what we are *now*," dark-haired Chris says. "But famous Chrises are an ancient goblin tradition and a longstanding position of prestige. I've been, among others, sixteenth-century English playwright Christopher Marlowe. God, I miss writers being the rock stars of popular culture, you know? I didn't do a single sit-up for like three centuries."

Australian Chris laughs. "Yeah, I feel you. When I was elected to the Council, I was Christopher of Bavaria, King of Sweden, Denmark, and Norway. Man, royals were *it* back then. I wish that had carried over into the New World. Royals eat all the carbs they want."

"Same here," starship-captain Chris laments. "I was Christopher the First of Denmark *and* Christopher the Second of Denmark. You think people are stupid and oblivious now? Lemme tell you . . ."

Lena nods, her head spinning more than a little. She looks to formerly fat Chris expectantly.

"Oh, I'm new," he says. "This is my first Chris."

"So, which one of you was Columbus?" Lena asks.

All four of their faces darken, and each Chris looks away awkwardly.

Bronko leans down and whispers in her ear, "Columbus was more'n a bit of a dick, even by goblin standards. He's considered a blight on the Chris name, if you will."

Lena rolls her eyes.

"Listen, we needed the King's help," Bronko tells them. "My people did his family a solid once. Those same people are facin' hard times, and more, and I was hopin' the King would want to repay that small service by helping us out."

"Well, the way I heard it," starship-captain Chris says haughtily, "and granted, I was on location in Europe at the time, your catering company turned every human at the King's son's wedding into ravenous lizard monsters that nearly killed every goblin there."

"I suppose it depends a whole lot on your proximity and perspective," Bronko offers diplomatically.

"Can you at least put us in touch with the King?" Lena asks, her blood beginning to rise.

"*Former* King," Starship Chris corrects her. "And no, he's incommunicado. Any formal requests you have need to go through the Council."

Lena has to stop grinding her teeth to ask, "Then can *you* help us?"

None of the Chrises answers her. They all seem suddenly preoccupied with scouring the fronts of their sweaters for errant lint.

"You know what's happening out there, don't you?" Ritter says, and it's not really a question. "Who reached out to you? The new Allensworth . . . or the old Allensworth?"

"Our official policy is to keep *all* diplomatic channels open," Australian Chris states vaguely.

"Look, guys," Bronko all but pleads, "I know who I am, all right? I'm a has-been cable TV chef who wasn't never pretty enough to be mistaken for no goblin. And we're just a bunch of cooks and workaday magicians. But we've served all y'all for years. My people, they're *good* people. They're caught in the crosshairs of something big here, and it ain't their fault. Whatever . . . 'civil unrest' may be comin', and whatever side y'all take, I just don't

want my people to be collateral damage. I'm not askin'
you to bleed. Just the word gettin' out that we're under
your protection might make all the difference for us with
what's to come."

The Chrises confer silently with one another, and
despite being pissed at all of them now, Lena can't
help being more than a little hypnotized by the stares
they're exchanging. Each pair of those eyes is just so
damn inviting.

"We can't be involved, Chef," Australian Chris de-
crees. "I'm sorry for your predicament. Truly, I am. However, we four are entrusted with the welfare of *our* people,
and with the state of the world around us in such flux
right now, above and beneath the surface, it behooves us
to remain neutral until we get a proper lay of the land. I'm
sure you understand."

"Yeah," Bronko says tightly. "I get it."

"I don't," Lena says without reservation.

Ritter fills in the blank without emotion. "They don't
want to do anything to piss off Allensworth in case he
wins."

"Yeah, well," starship-captain Chris says hurriedly. "Is
there anything *else* we can do for you, Chef?"

"Can't think of a thing," Bronko answers in a mock-
ingly pleasant tone.

"We wish you luck," Australian Chris offers. "I hope to

see those Colorado chili poppers at an event again someday."

With that, three of the Chrises turn and exit the way they came.

Formerly fat Chris, the youngest and newest among them, lingers a moment.

"Sorry," he says sheepishly before joining the rest of the Council.

Lena watches them go, less impressed by celebrity than she's ever been in her life. Her stomach feels as though it's collapsing.

"I just wish I could Facebook this," she says bitterly.

# UNDER THE HAZING MOON

Moon spends almost fifteen minutes attempting to scrub, scrape, and finally chisel the plate clean before declaring it unsalvageable and discarding it. The cheap plastic dish clatters loudly against a dozen others just like it when Moon drops it into the trash can. He's managed to restore perhaps half his dinnerware, and each piece he's lost to the fossilized remnants of Chinese takeout food is just another reason for him to eventually purchase grown-up plates and bowls, and possibly even glasses that are actually made of glass.

The rest of Moon's Jamaica walk-up has been almost completely transformed. There isn't a single scrap of clothing on what Moon was surprised to be reminded are hardwood floors. The surfaces of all the furniture are largely exposed; the usual array of empty food containers and wrappers, and excessive amounts of head-shop gear, have all been swept away and carried out in bulging garbage bags. Moon has even gone so far as to dust and vacuum.

He hasn't neglected himself, either. Moon took all of the clothes he collected from their various lonely piles and spent the afternoon at the coin laundry around the corner. It may in fact be the first time the *Gears of War* shirt he's wearing has been clean since he bought it. It took Moon far less time with a plastic comb to tame his perpetual bedhead into something largely resembling a third-grader on their first day of school.

He's preparing to break the seal on a new bottle of lemon Pledge when he hears someone knocking. Moon snaps the vinyl gloves from each of his small hands and exits the kitchen, jogging across the uncluttered floor of his living room to answer the front door.

Ritter, Marcus, and Cindy are waiting at the top of the long cement steps leading to Moon's front door. Marcus is shouldering what looks like a heavily weighted messenger's bag.

"Oh," Moon says, clearly caught off guard. "Shit."

Marcus looks at the others. "He must mean you two. I'm a delight to find at your front door, even for strangers."

"Inspection time, Moon," Ritter says seriously.

Moon's eyebrows shoot up. "What? For real?"

"Of course not, boy," Cindy barks at him. "You ain't in the Army. Now step aside like a civilized somebody so we can come in."

Moon shuffles back away from the door and the trio enter.

"Well, I'll be cot-damned," Cindy marvels, taking in the space.

Not only is the apartment nearly spotless, Moon's shrine to video gaming is gone. In fact, he doesn't even seem to own a television anymore. Several poorly assembled IKEA bookcases have replaced the battalion of consoles and speakers and assorted electronic paraphernalia. The bookcases are sparsely populated with graphic novels of Japanese origin, most of them with uncracked spines that look brand-new.

"The kids appreciated the gift," Ritter informs Moon when he notices the change.

"I figured it was the best way to get rid of the stuff."

"Where's the fucked-up cherub?" Cindy asks.

"Cupid? He, uh, bailed," Moon explains distractedly, busy fluffing and rearranging the pillows on his duct-taped yet immaculately vacuumed and brushed futon. "I guess he felt the heat comin' down, didn't want any."

"Where did he go?" Ritter asks.

Moon shrugs. "Who knows? He's an interdimensional demon assassin. I'm sure he's got other couches he can crash on. I gave him what was left of our weed stash and wished him luck."

"Sorry you lost your roommate," Cindy says.

Moon shrugs. "It was probably time. All we did was what-do-you-call-it . . . *enable* each other."

Cindy whistles. "That's some high-concept shit for you, Moon. And look at you. You look like Eminem at a bail hearing. You're evolving right before our dang eyes."

Moon shifts uncomfortably. "Yeah. I didn't expect you guys . . . and girl," he adds quickly, "to come here."

"Bronko said we had to see this for ourselves."

"And Ryland told us you've been an apt pupil lately," Ritter adds.

"Is that what he said?" Marcus asks. "I can't understand shit through that guy's brogue. The booze slurring doesn't help either."

"I'm not doing any of it to kiss ass with you guys," Moon is quick to point out.

"Is that a fact?" Cindy asks, plopping onto the futon and spreading out languidly. "Damn, check me actually being able to sit down in this place, and without sticking to anything."

Moon ignores the shade. "Yeah, it was something Bronko said."

Ritter is inspired to grin, just a little. "He has that habit, doesn't he?"

Moon nods. "Yeah, well, what he said made sense to me. I needed to hear it, I guess."

"Well, that shit worked, whatever it was," Cindy remarks.

Moon smiles. However, it's an expression of sorrow.

It's as if he's already accepted the answer is no when he asks, "You think you can ever forgive me, Cin?"

She cocks her head. "I ain't heard you apologize yet."

"I'm sorry I lied to y'all. I'm sorry for all the times I made shit harder than it needed to be, and didn't take stuff seriously, and all the times I . . . I just didn't try. I guess I just thought . . . I got used to people using me for whatever this thing is I was born with, y'know? My old man and every bar owner down south who ever put me up and fed me free beer for the action I brought into their place. You're not like that. You're not like them, but I didn't . . . like, let myself *know* that, or whatever."

As he speaks, Cindy leans forward on the futon, resting her forearms atop her knees and regarding him perhaps more seriously than she ever has.

"Well, that was some deeper ish than I ever expected outta you, Moon," she admits.

"What about Hara?" Ritter asks him.

Moon's expression hardens. "Hara wasn't my fault, dude. I'm always gonna be sorry I couldn't help him. He was my bro. But I didn't kill him."

Ritter nods. "That's right, you didn't. I just wanted to make sure you knew that."

Moon begins blinking as if tears are threatening his eyes. He looks away briefly, then back at the three of them, clearing his throat.

Cindy stands. "Look here, I ain't about to forgive you in your admittedly defunkified apartment, but I *am* willing to let you roll with us and earn it. We need you. We needed you before, and we need you even more now for what's coming at us."

Something like a smile, albeit a tormented one, touches Moon's lips.

"Thanks, Cin."

Moon's gaze shifts to Marcus, seeming to be waiting for something from Ritter's brother.

Marcus stares back at him indifferently for a moment and then seems to realize Moon is awaiting some kind of verdict from him.

"Oh, this is all you guys," he says. "I don't have an opinion. I'm only here cuz I wanted to watch."

Moon looks from him to Ritter and Cindy. "Watch what?"

Marcus hauls the satchel slung from his shoulder in front of his stomach, unzipping the bag and reaching inside.

Moon's eyes widen as he watches Marcus remove from the satchel a gallon plastic Ziploc bag filled with large misshapen lumps that have been battered, seasoned, and fried. The resulting pepper-speckled golden-brown skin looks familiar to Moon, even if the shape and size of the "food" items do not.

"Wait," he says, pointing at the bag. "Are those—"

"One of the last official batches of Chicken Nuggies distributed by the now defunct Henley's Fast Food Corporation," Cindy confirms.

Moon's mouth hangs open for a moment before he says, "But that means . . . that means those are . . ."

She nods triumphantly. "Fried pieces of the sumbitch genie I dick-punted into that fryer my very own self."

Moon looks up at Ritter who shrugs without a readable expression on his face.

"Where did you even get those?" Moon asks.

"eBay," Marcus says. "I also got some of that special limited edition 'Szechwan' sauce. I've been posting pics all week on threads of whiny-ass *Rick and Morty* fans complaining about not getting any of me feeding it to squirrels and giving it to homeless dudes. It's awesome."

The part of Moon he hasn't scrubbed away with cleansers can't help snickering at that, at least until a new thought sobers him up.

"Wait . . . what do you want me to do?"

"Consider it a welcome-back initiation," Cindy advises him with a cattish grin.

Marcus bangs his head as if he's in the mosh pit of a metal concert and holds up the sign of the Devil with his free hand.

"You guys suck so hard," Moon says, but his grin almost matches hers.

"Less talking, more choking down all this bad juju," Marcus demands. "I want to see what it does to you, or what *you* do to *it*. I've heard some bananas stories about you and a live leprechaun."

Moon's grin tightens. "Yeah," he says quietly, looking up at Ritter. "I guess we do have some stories, huh?"

Ritter nods, the faintest smile on his lips. "That we do."

Moon takes a deep breath. "All right, fuck it. Bring it on. I'll get a clean plate."

"You got any clean plates?" Cindy asks with a raised eyebrow.

"They're *all* clean," Moon proudly announces.

# DESPERATE MEASURES

Bronko fills the bottom of two glasses on his desktop with whiskey older than he is and offers Ritter a cigar from a box of pre-embargo Cubans.

"If you're trying to get in my pants, boss," Ritter says dryly as he carefully removes one of the stogies, "you don't have to wine and dine me like this."

It's late into the evening, and Bronko has summoned Ritter to his office clandestinely, instructing him not to tell any of the others.

"Think of it more like the pit master feedin' a gladiator the finest mead and elk in the larder before a fight."

Ritter makes a noise almost like a laugh but without the mirth.

They both bite the ends off of their respective cigars and spit them into a large ashtray Bronko brought out with the rest. He lights their stogies and the two of them puff exultantly.

"Small pleasures," Bronko affirms.

He picks up his whiskey tumbler, and Ritter follows suit.

Bronko raises his glass across the desk. "You're a good man, Ritt. I'm sorry as hell I ever offered you this job, but I'm damn glad you took it."

Ritter elevates his tumbler. "Nowhere else I'd rather be, all things considered. And thank you, boss. I won't insult you by disagreeing."

Bronko nods. "Good policy."

They toast, then drink down the hundred-year-old whiskey, savoring it for as long as they can resist the burn.

Ritter places his empty glass on the desktop and puffs on his cigar.

"So, we did that. Now tell me."

Bronko takes a deep, pensive breath. "We need to know for sure if Allensworth is still alive. And if he is, we need proof of what he's been doin' to take to Consoné and the Sceadu. We don't know why, but we know for damn certain he tried to ruin Consoné's shot at Sceadu President, and we know he tried to use Vargas to assassinate him, but our word alone ain't enough. If we can prove he's a direct threat to them, they'll have to intervene. It's the only way to keep everyone safe. Callin' it favors ain't gonna cut it, especially with the goblins turnin' their backs on us. If we can't get the Sceadu to take him on, he'll crush us."

Ritter nods. "Makes sense, but we don't even know

where to start looking for him, let alone hard evidence of whatever he's planning."

"I do," Bronko says resolutely, taking a deep puff of his cigar and languidly exhaling to steady his nerves.

Ritter places his stogie in the ashtray and leans forward, listening intently.

"He . . . Allensworth . . . he took me out to this cabin once, upstate." Bronko leans back in his chair, sighing. "It wasn't a Sceadu joint or any kind of government-spook safe house. It was *his* place. It was private, had a ton of heat around it. His guys, I'm sure. I don't think anyone else knows about it. Hell, I don't think he really thought much of me being there. I am just a damn ol' cook, after all. But it strikes me it'd be a good place to look for secrets, and I'm pretty sure I remember how to find it."

Ritter nods. "Tell me where."

Bronko holds up a hand. "Hold on there, hoss. This ain't like any job I've ever given y'all. This here ain't about business, or for a client or some damn catering event. This is off the grid, and it's the worst kind of dangerous. If it goes ass-up, you *will* get yourselves killed, and maybe worse."

Ritter doesn't hesitate. "Like I said, tell me where."

Bronko grins crookedly. "Rest of your team'll feel the same, will they?"

"I think I can guarantee it."

"All right, then."

Bronko leans forward, taking a piece of paper out of a drawer along with a pen.

He pauses and then looks at Ritter with a dark expression on his face.

"One more thing," he says. "You're going there to look for evidence we can use against him. It may be he's laid up there himself. Probably not, but it could be. If he *is* there . . . you kill him, ya hear?"

Ritter's eyes harden. "I'm not an assassin, boss."

"No, you ain't, and I ain't askin' you to be. I'm not offering to pay you. I'd do it my damn self if I could get my hands around his throat. This is self-defense, self-preservation. That's why you do it. Hell, kill him for your own reasons. You have enough of 'em."

Ritter nods.

"You're right," he says. "I do."

# TWO DARRENS, ONE BEWITCHED

White Horse's chanting is the sound of the past disagreeing with the future, something deep and ancient, not of this time and unsuited for the modern world. His faded jeans-covered legs are crossed beside the plain mattress laid on the floor of the subterranean chamber beneath Sin du Jour that houses Ritter's Stocking & Receiving department. Darren's shirtless, comatose body is resting atop the mattress, Little Dove gently dabbing the sweat from his forehead with a damp cloth, her young brow furrowed in concern. James crouches at the foot of the makeshift sickbed, his arm still cradled in a sling, his anguished gaze solely for Darren.

Smoke fills the windowless room, acrid and white, wafting from the singed sprig of herbs pinched between White Horse's fingertips. He waves the thin, burning stalks over Darren's body, continuing to chant low and slow and steady.

"It smells like spaghetti in here," Cindy comments.

Ritter glowers at her quietly.

"Well, it does!"

He and what remains of his team are watching from a distance with Lena, who ignores the pair's brief exchange, focusing on Darren, who hasn't truly been awake since they rescued him from Allensworth's clutches at Gluttony Bay. Since their return, they've kept Darren sedated until White Horse and Little Dove returned to drive out whatever evil influence was poured into him to enact Allensworth's plot to assassinate the new President of the Sceadu.

"Pop, is that sage?" Little Dove asks White Horse.

"It's parsley," the old man informs her between his thrumming refrains.

"Pop!"

"It doesn't matter!" White Horse snaps, ceasing to chant completely. "How many times do I need to tell you that?"

"How can it not matter?"

"It's like lighting a fire. What difference does it make what you use for kindling?"

"I mean, you can use a million chemicals to start a fire too, but if they're the wrong ones, you'll blow the building up."

"That's why I said the thing I said the way I said it."

"If it doesn't matter, how does any of this crap work?"

"Haven't you learned anything?"

"You haven't really been heavy on procedure."

"That's because there is no 'procedure.' It all comes from the Hatałii, and from the spirit world they call upon." The old man holds up the smoldering parsley sprig. "*This* is a tradition. It's just a way to connect us to ourselves. It's how we separate what we do from the normal flow of this world. It doesn't matter what herb you burn. It's not fucking Harry Potter."

"At least Harry Potter has rules!"

"Will you please not argue with each other?" James asks them both, calmly. "Not now."

"Sorry," Little Dove grumbles.

White Horse returns to his chanting and his ministrations.

"How long will it take to heal him?" Lena finally asks from the background, trying to stem her growing frustration.

"I can't heal his spirit. Only he can do that."

"What do you mean?" Lena demands. "This is, like, an exorcism, right? Why can't you just pull whatever was controlling him out so we can kill it?"

"There's nothing inside him," White Horse insists, obviously growing impatient with her ignorance. "There's no demon controlling him. It's just him. Whatever spoke to his spirit split it in two, you understand? It created another Darren, one that's everything . . . dark and hateful in his soul. I've seen it before. They played on his fears, on his hatred of who he is. He poisoned himself."

"Then how are you going to help him?" Lena asks, her voice edging into desperation, the pain and fear and regret beginning to sound through unchecked.

"I'm going to call him out," White Horse answers.

Lena opens her mouth to question the old man further, but Ritter gently grips her wrist. When she looks up at him, Ritter shakes his head.

"Please, can you bring him back to me now?" James asks White Horse, his abject serenity given away only by the tears welling in his eyes. "I have waited long enough."

"It's white people magic took 'im from us and from himself," the Hatałii assures the young chef. "They don't know who they're fucking with."

White Horse blows hot, extinguishing breath through the smoking herbs and sets them aside. He leans back, squaring his shoulders and closing his eyes. His arms slowly rise above his shoulders.

"Shit," Little Dove breathes quietly.

She knows what comes next.

When White Horse begins chanting anew, his voice is utterly changed. The entire atmosphere of the space around them changes with it, or perhaps is altered by that voice. The temperature and barometric pressure drop, prickling all of their skins. The old man's chanting is deeper, booming, echoing beyond the simple acoustics of the cement room. It's a voice that isn't speaking to them; it's calling to forces beyond their mortal plane, a voice strong enough to rip through the membrane of our reality and reach the souls that have gone beyond. Wind that shouldn't exist in a room with no windows and a locked door rises around them, sweeping back and forth as White Horse's chanting continues to grow in depth and power and volume.

"This is some hoodoo-type shit here!" Cindy yells above the sudden chaos.

"This is nothing!" Marcus insists. "We watched this brujo snake-handling dude once—"

"Shut up, Marc!" Ritter instructs him.

He keeps hold of Lena's wrist as she takes a step forward, watching Darren begin to stir, then thrash from side to side atop the mattress. Little Dove does her best to keep him still without harming him, but his convulsions become more violent. A deep, thrumming moan of pain emanates from his throat that soon causes him to begin frothing at the mouth.

"You are harming him!" James shouts against the chants of the old man. "Please, stop! Can you not see he is in pain?"

"Just wait!" Little Dove instructs him, struggling with every ounce of her strength to help control Darren's agonized throes.

White Horse's demigod voice reaches the earsplitting pinnacle of its crescendo, and as it does, it's as if a deafening thunderclap explodes above their heads in the water-stained concrete of the ceiling.

Then all is silence.

It takes a moment from all of them to recover their senses in the wake of the crash. It takes another moment after that for all of them to realize there is a new addition to the room.

Darren, another Darren, is standing at the foot of the mattress, looking down on his other self with disgust.

"Look at him, the pendejo."

He's a Xerox of Darren save for his wide, alert eyes and dry skin, but his voice and manner possess nothing the rest of them have come to know of the man. He's like an actor who plays Darren breaking character to reveal his contempt for that character.

"You know, in high school, he wouldn't even jerk off because he was afraid someone would find out he was thinking about the dude from that old *Hercules* show? How crazy is that, being scared someone will find out what you're *thinking*?"

"He had plenty of reasons to be afraid back then," Lena says, almost like a reflex, ignoring the surreal absurdity of the situation.

"But he never stopped! Fucking coward."

James stands slowly, moving his gaze up and down the other Darren.

"You are not my amour."

"I'm not a fag," the projection fires back at him.

"Neither is he," James responds coolly.

White Horse rests a hand as old and leathery as a weathered saddle on the real Darren's forehead.

"Open your eyes, son," the Hatałii whispers into his ear. "We've pulled your spirit free of 'im. Now you have to face him, face yourself, and take him back into you purified. You have to do that to be whole again. You have to reconcile all that horseshit we all carry around, weighting our spirits like damn anchor chain. You can't let it be separate from you anymore."

The other Darren laughs. "You writing a fucking Emily Dickinson poem down there, old man?"

White Horse looks to James, who seems to read the message in the old man's eyes with total clarity. James turns his back on the poisonous projection at the foot of the bed and kneels beside Darren's true form. He takes the hand of his unconscious lover and covers it with both of his.

"It is time to come back to me," James tells him. "It is time to be you again, to be us again. Please, mon amour."

"Open your eyes, son," White Horse repeats. "You've put this off too long."

Little Dove lightly rests her fingertips against Darren's

temple, closing her eyes and summoning whatever power to which she's become attuned, hoping she can will it to reinforce her friend's spirit and resolve and strength.

Tremors wrinkle Darren's eyelids, each one weighted heavily as they strain to open.

"He can't get rid of me," his other self insists.

"He doesn't need to," White Horse whispers without looking at the poisonous projection.

The true Darren's eyelids snap back and he gasps like a drowning man breaking clear of the water's surface. His back arches above the bed, Little Dove stroking his chest and stomach and whispering calmly in his ear that he's all right. When Darren sees himself, really sees the projection of his own self-loathing and all of his hate and malice, he's at first shocked, then repulsed.

"Don't look away," White Horse urges him.

"That's all he does!" the other Darren shouts.

Tears begin filling the true Darren's eyes, his features contorting in an expression of absolute misery and deep emotional pain.

"Please, mon ami, do as Mr. White Horse says and do not look away," James pleads with him. "Be strong."

"I can't," Darren manages through the wracking sobs that follow.

"You can!" James insists.

"Please!" Darren tearfully begs.

"Do you see?" the other version of him addresses them all in disgust. "Do you see how he is?"

"Look at him, mon ami!" James finally shouts at the true Darren. "Do it now! He is *nothing*! There is only you!"

It looks as if Darren is trying to swallow broken glass. He moans painfully as he forces a measure of control over his tormented face. He blinks hard, steeling himself.

"That's it, man," Lena quietly urges him. "Come on . . ."

Darren shuts his eyes tight, but when he opens them again, it's to stare up at the darkest part of him given form.

"I know you," Darren says to him, voice raspy and shaking.

"You don't know shit, cabrón. It's all that white blood in you. It's like pouring piss into motor oil."

"I know you," Darren repeats, louder, his voice firmer.

"That's right, son," White Horse says. "It's time."

"Time for what?" the other Darren shouts down at them. "What's he going to do?"

"I know you," Darren repeats, adding, "and I know who I am. And I'm not going back to sleep. I've slept enough."

The other Darren hesitates for the first time. Then, a darkness filling the projection's eyes until they're almost

73

black, he whispers, "What are you without me?"

Darren swallows, hard, staring at his worst self coldly.

"Free," he says.

There is no visual spectacle to accompany the conclusion, no rising score or special effects, as there would be in a movie. The other Darren doesn't scream a deathly, otherworldly scream as he's sucked back into the real Darren's body and absorbed by his renewed spirit.

The projection simply blinks out of existence. One moment, there are two Darrens, and in the next, there is only the one lying atop the mattress.

No one speaks at first, not until Darren asks White Horse, "Is that it? Did I . . . Is it done?"

"You did good, boy," White Horse assures him. "You did something most people never do, not in their whole lives. You're gonna be fine."

Darren tries to smile, but the smile quickly turns to tears. He tries to close his eyes, but nothing can stem the torrent that overtakes him in the next moment.

Fortunately, James is there. He covers Darren like a medic's blanket after a disaster, cupping his face in his hands and kissing Darren's forehead and lips.

"It is okay," he whispers. "Now is the time for tears. Do not be ashamed."

"I'm sorry," Darren manages in one wet, ragged breath. "I hurt you—"

"You did nothing," James insists. "You killed the man who hurt me and you. Now there is only us. We will speak of it no more."

Darren relents, clinging to him as if James is the lone piece of driftwood in storm-wracked waters, and James holds him close. As they embrace, Lena and the others stand over them, Darren's best friend of so many years holding back her own tears as she watches him find a much-needed measure of grace in the arms of what may be his first true love.

"Welcome back, champ," Ritter says.

Sitting back from the commiserating, White Horse realizes his granddaughter is staring up at him with an odd expression on her face.

"What is it?" he asks.

"I still have a lot to learn from you, don't I?"

White Horse makes a tired sound hoping to approximate laughter. "Some things only time can teach. And most of those times, you only learn by falling on your ass and failing everyone. I've done more'n my share of that. Believe it. You've taught me more these past few months than I'll ever teach you, trust me."

"I do," his granddaughter tells him.

White Horse doesn't know what to say to that, or how to explain to her the long-abandoned feelings within him those words stir. He falls silent, and for a time the only sound echoing throughout the cement room is Darren crying. It lasts until he has no more tears left, but no one seems to mind waiting. Everyone in this subbasement chamber has learned that's what life is largely, waiting for the tears to pass so you can move on to the next.

# CABIN IN THE WOODS

"Can I just say that watching her work is like watching Rembrandt paint, only I want to have sex with this Rembrandt?" Marcus asks his older brother, lowering the night vision binoculars through which he had been viewing the world.

"Even if she weren't my best friend, that would still be ridiculously offensive," Ritter dryly replies.

"Fine, whatever, so I won't *tweet* it. Jesus."

Marcus mutters unintelligibly, returning to his night vision specs.

Moon snickers. "Dude, it's awesome hearing Ritter give someone besides me shit for a change."

The three of them are crouching in the underbrush of a forest about fifteen miles outside Tuxedo, New York. The cabin they're surveying is more of a lodge, large and opulent and filling the center of a broad clearing. A paved drive has been laid through the woods and winds up to the front door. A more modern structure set several dozen yards off to the right of the cabin serves as what appears to be a guardhouse and barracks for a battalion-sized security force. They look human, albeit heavily armed. The only other occupants of the property are the ruins of an ancient-looking well behind the cabin.

Marcus digs at his ear. "This wax itches like a bastard."

"Yeah," Moon seconds. "Why are we wearing these earplugs, again?"

"The same reason you're wearing contacts spun from Franciscan church glass. I have no idea what kind of magic is protecting that cabin, but knowing Allensworth, it's powerful and nasty. Eyes and ears are the easiest things to fool and assault. If you're up for possibly having blood shoot out of your fucking ears until your head explodes, by all means, take out the sacred wax plugs I made myself."

"You could've just said 'protection' and I would've been cool," Moon mutters.

The bushes ahead of them rattle just a hair, and Marcus drops his specs to take up his heavy-gauge shotgun.

Cindy crawls from the bushes deftly, parting from the shadows into which she's perfectly blended, decked out from head to toe in pitch-black.

Marcus lowers the shotgun, grinning cattishly as she peels back the hood covering her face.

"I wired the well to blow remotely," she informs them, wiping grass and dirt from her sleek tactical gear, "and then I set a break all the way back to the tree line."

"What's a break?" Moon asks.

"It's a series of charges that'll funnel whatever force trips the first charge into the next and then the next and so on. Only, I set the break to push those goons *away* from the cabin. Once they all hustle over to the well and trip the first charge, it should give us plenty of time while they're dealing with all those fireworks."

"Why didn't you just wire the guardhouse and get 'em all at once?" Moon persists.

Cindy gives him a look of disdain. "Because I ain't a damn mass murderer, for one. And even if I didn't mind flat-out killin' several dozen people, there's no way I could've gotten close enough with all of them in there. It was hard enough crawling through the grass like some damn ninja."

"Sorry," Moon says.

Cindy looks to Ritter. "Let's work around to the front and get in position, and I'll light this candle."

He nods, motioning to Marcus and Moon.

The foursome stealthily moves between the trees, slowly rounding the interior edge of the clearing to circumvent the huge edifice of the cabin.

"Probably ain't the time," Cindy says lowly to Ritter as they go, "but it occurs to me, things being things and all, this might be our last mission. Even if we don't get ourselves fragged. It feels like . . . I don't know, the end is coming one way or the other."

Ritter smiles sorrowfully in the dark. "They were never missions, Cin. We deliver food for a catering company."

"You know what I mean, man," she snaps in her typically impatient way.

"Yeah," he says, and there's a lot held in that simple word if one knows Ritter well, "I do."

"We damn sure did the things," she says.

"Yeah, we did."

"You two need a moment, or a room?" Marcus asks.

"Why?" Cindy shoots back at him wryly. "You wanna watch? Got you pegged as a freak, anyway."

Again, he grins. "You don't even know. But you'll find out."

"I think they call this 'creating a hostile work environment,'" Moon comments.

Ritter halts, holding up a hand.

The chatter dies and their expressions all turn serious.

Ritter points beyond the brush. From their vantage, they can see the ornate front doors of the cabin. There are two sentries stationed there, both armed with automatic rifles.

"Do we know if Allensworth is at home?" Cindy asks.

Ritter shakes his head. "We don't even know for sure if he's still alive."

She looks at him intently. "What if he is? And what if he is?"

"We'll deal with it," he says vaguely.

Cindy frowns, knowing he has deeper thoughts on the matter but not pressing him.

"What do we do if they don't buck when she lights the well?" Marcus asks Ritter. "I didn't bring a sniper."

"Improvise" is all he says, nodding to Cindy.

She nods back, removing a small cylindrical remote control concealed inside her tac vest and flipping the safety guard from the trigger.

"We did the things," she repeats, smiling as bitter-sweetly as Ritter did a moment before.

He nods, returning the gesture.

Cindy presses the trigger. They can't see the crumbling old well blow, but they hear it like rippling thunder in the clearing. A moment later, stone shrapnel of varying sizes and shapes begins raining over the cabin, the sentries guarding the front entrance shrinking back as the debris clears the roof and pelts the paved drive in front of them.

"Fucking hell, Cin," Moon says.

She shrugs. "I wanted to get their attention."

They watch the sentries. They're both pressing gloved fingers to the communications devices in their ears, speaking frantically to whoever is listening at the other end.

"They're not abandoning their post," Marcus observes.

"Doesn't matter," Ritter says. "The guardhouse should be emptying right now. And they'll set off Cindy's break any—"

As if in answer to him, they hear a series of violent pops followed by chaotic screams issuing from the other side of the cabin.

Cindy can't help grinning.

"All right," Ritter says. "Let's do this. Stay behind me until I neutralize the sentries."

"How?" Marcus demands.

Ritter doesn't answer him. Instead, he pushes up the sleeve of his dark jacket, revealing a gold bracelet around his wrist forged in the shape of a serpent the trained eye would recognize as the god Ananke. He breaks from the bushes and charges across the clearing, rotating sections of the bracelet's serpentine body as he moves.

As the others watch in alarm, the sentries spot Ritter and both of them immediately raise their rifles, sighting on the sprinting figure easily and opening fire.

Before any of them can yell a warning to Ritter, however, the flashes of the sentries' muzzles seem to freeze and the report of their shots is silenced. The sentries themselves also appear to be frozen in place, and even the smoke still issuing from the fiery debris at their feet ceases to waft, as if time has somehow stopped.

Ritter finishes closing the gap between the edge of

the clearing and the front entrance. He leaps into the air without slowing down, spinning his body and driving the flat of his right foot into the chest of one of the sentries. The petrified guard flies backward, colliding with the double doors behind him and smashing them both open. Ritter lands gracefully and drops down low, sweeping the ankles of the other sentry, planking the man on the cabin porch. Ritter stands and raises his right leg until it's almost parallel with his torso and drives down the heel of his boot hard enough to shatter the sentry's chin.

"Fuckin' show-off," Marcus says as he, Cindy, and Moon break cover and run to join Ritter.

Ritter quickly rearranges the serpentine sections of his bracelet and covers it with his sleeve. He reaches inside his jacket pockets and removes two smooth, plain, light-colored stones. Stepping just past the threshold exposed by the wrecked doors, Ritter slams the bottoms of both stones together, the clap echoing throughout the darkened, cavernous space inside and causing the air to imperceptibly ripple.

"Damn, you gutted your home security system, didn't you?" Marcus says to him as the three of them finish their job to the porch.

Ritter nods, stashing the stones in his pockets. "That should neutralize any magical devices inside, unless he's got something nuclear-powered."

"Then let's do this."

Marcus racks the heavy slide of his shotgun, like an affirmation.

They can still hear Cindy's break charges exploding in the distance as they enter, the sounds moving farther and farther back toward the clearing.

A marble foyer lights up automatically as its sensors detect their presence, followed by a great room beyond. Far from being rustic, the cabin's interior is more like a Napoleonic palace than a lodge in the middle of the rural countryside.

"Even with your magic-killing rock whatever thing," Moon ponders, "I expected this dude's shit to be locked down heavier than this, didn't you?"

"The little stoner has a point," Marcus says. "Dozens of heavily armed Blackwater rejects aside, this seems pretty easy."

"Bite me, new guy," Moon fires back.

"Don't speak too soon," Cindy warns them.

As if on cue, the sound of large paws skittering across the great room floor draws their attention.

A large Rottweiler trots up to the edge of the marble foyer, its tongue hanging out as it regards them passively.

"Shit," Ritter whispers. "Bruno."

"What?" Marcus asks, confused. "It's just a fucking dog."

"No, it's not," his brother assures him.

"You're getting old, man." Marcus snaps his fingers at the Rottweiler. "Fuck off, pooch, we're busy."

Bruno blinks at him then leaps up to stand on his hind legs.

The growl that issues from his maw in the next moment does not belong to a household canine. It's the ferocious bellow of something colossal and ancient and hungry. The dog's body begins morphing to match his voice, its mass doubling, then tripling in size. Its jaws extend and widen until they're large enough to encompass a grown man's head whole. In moments, a canine-like creature that is a head taller than any of them and rippling with muscle is gnashing knife-like teeth at them, his eyes glowing as red as brimstone.

"Oh, fuck me!" Marcus curses, raising his shotgun and firing.

The first blast hits the creature in his side, and he shrugs it off with little effort. Marcus racks the slide and pumps two more rounds into the monstrous canine, only serving to momentarily falter his step and further piss him off.

"Seriously?" Cindy shouts, rearing back and throwing her tomahawk at the beast.

Her aim is true, and the blade of the axe's curved head buries itself deep in the monster's chest, but once again, it only causes the creature to howl in rage and continue to advance on them all.

Ritter calmly reaches into the right pants pocket and removes an orange shotgun shell. With equal calmness, he offers it to his brother.

"Here," he says.

Marcus blinks at the shell, hesitating for a moment before finally reaching out and taking it. With far less serenity than his brother, he begins hastily loading it into the shotgun's feeding tube.

"Faster is better," Ritter says, watching the towering beast close the gap between them, six-inch claws and dripping fangs flashing in the light of the foyer.

Marcus shoves the shell into the tube with the tip of his thumb and quickly racks the slide.

Bruno rears back on his haunches and lunges directly at Ritter, its roar deafening and its maw spreading as wide and black as the mouth of a volcano.

Marcus puts the butt of the weapon to his shoulder and pulls the trigger, filling the foyer and great room with thunder.

A near-seven-foot Rottweiler crashes to the marble floor at Ritter's feet, motionless, its coat smoking where Marcus's blast tore through it.

Ritter seems to finally exhale, although none of them could tell he was holding his breath. He gently prods the beast with the toe of his boot.

"Dead?" his brother asks.

Ritter nods. "Or very, very sleepy."

Marcus discharges the shell that killed the creature, reloading the shotgun.

"What was in that shell?" he asks Ritter.

"A dollar-eighty in Mercury dimes. Ninety percent silver."

"Does that thing count as a werewolf?" Moon asks.

Ritter shrugs. "Close enough."

Cindy rips her tomahawk blade from Bruno's chest. "Well, that was all kinds of fucked."

"None of you should be here."

Marcus spins around and levels his shotgun, his right index finger slipping past the guard to tickle the trigger.

It's Luciana Monrovio, Allensworth's former (and supposedly deceased) succubus assistant. She's wearing a creaseless canary-yellow skirt suit. Her pumps and the oversized frames of her eyeglasses match the color perfectly.

She's watching them all with a heavy look of judgment on her angular face.

"Where the fuck did you come from?" Cindy asks, genuinely shocked at the woman's sudden presence.

"I repeat," Luciana says stiffly, "none of you should be here. This is Mr. Allensworth's private residence." She peers down at Bruno. "And you've murdered his favorite pet."

"So, the bastard is still kicking," Cindy says. "Allensworth, I mean."

"Oh, Mr. Allensworth is quite well, I assure you, and very much looking forward to seeing you all again."

Cindy looks at Ritter. "I thought Lena said she stuck a butcher's knife through this bitch's mug."

Ritter nods without comment, scrutinizing Luciana closely.

Her face, neck, and skull are all unblemished. Her dark hair is perfectly coiffed. She appears to be the exact opposite of someone who was stabbed under the chin with a very large blade.

"Weapons free?" Marcus asks Ritter, ready to open fire on the succubus.

Ritter shakes his head. "I think you'd be wasting the shot, little brother."

He picks up a small yet surprisingly heavy decorative snuffbox from a nearby side table and tosses it at Luciana.

The object enters her abdomen and passes through her as if she's not even there, breaking open on the cabin floor behind her.

She frowns. "That was an antique, from the New Orleans brothel that once served as the Sceadu's early American headquarters."

"She's a fucking ghost?" Moon marvels.

"I am a noncorporeal human," Luciana corrects him.

Cindy shakes her head. "Damn, girl, you really are Evil Jett, aren't you?"

"Allensworth still has you on the dangle, even in death," Ritter says, and he sounds almost sympathetic to her plight.

"My contract extends beyond this mortal coil, and I am fortunate it does, believe me."

Ritter is quiet for a moment, his wheels turning, and then he says, "If you're here, then you're guarding something, and I'm guessing it's important."

"Is that why you've committed this act of breaking and entering, not to mention destruction of private property? In the vain hope of gaining some advantage over Mr. Allensworth?"

"Tell us where we can find proof of what he's planning," Ritter says calmly, "something we can present to the Sceadu. Help us and I'll find a way to free you, I promise."

Luciana laughs, and it's as though someone with secondhand knowledge once explained to her what laughing is supposed to sound like.

"My dear boy, I am quite happy with the terms of my current contract. I do not imagine I would fare well unbound on the other side of things."

"Being evil as fuck in life does that to a bitch," Cindy says with unabashed rancor.

Luciana stares dispassionately at her. "I am going to kill you all now," she pleasantly concludes. "Rest assured your colleagues at Sin du Jour will not linger behind for long."

From inside his jacket, Ritter quickly and deftly unfolds an old-fashioned Polaroid camera on a nylon strap and aims it at Luciana, the flash blinding them all as he snaps a picture of her.

When the gold-tinted veil over their vision parts, Luciana is gone.

Ritter removes the instant photograph produced by the camera and waves it briefly to help dry the image.

"That'll bind her for a while at least," he explains, tossing the photograph of Luciana staring into the camera hatefully across the room.

"You *do* come prepared, my brother," Marcus says with a grin.

"Impressive shit, dude," Moon adds.

Cindy rolls her eyes. "Oh, stop sucking his dick and let's get a move on. Those guards won't be fucking around with those charges forever."

Ritter conceals a grin of his own and walks through the high, broad arch on the other side of the great room. The space beyond illuminates automatically just as the foyer and great room did.

The space is dominated by a gargantuan slab of carved onyx serving as the top of a U-shaped desk. A rich, oxblood leather chair with a throne-like back rests between its flanks, and smaller chairs have been placed in front of it for visitors. The room's picture windows are totally covered by blackout curtains that appear thick enough to stop bullets.

"This must be the dude's office," Moon observes, obviously trying his best to come across as astute.

"Good catch, Moon," Cindy says sarcastically.

"What are we looking for?" Marcus asks his brother.

"Anything," Ritter answers, distracted. "Everything."

"Right."

Ritter scans the walls. There are several large oil paintings set in frames that probably cost as much as a midsize car. He recognizes a triptych by Bosch depicting the creation of the world, and imagines some museum curator believing they have anything other than a copy on *their* wall. Ritter begins to move slowly around Allensworth's desk, examining each object resting on the gleaming onyx surface. There are several slender, lethally sharp letter openers arranged atop a velvet cloth that look more like Masonic ceremonial daggers. There's a globe the size of a cantaloupe, made of glass, filled with what appears to be violet petals.

Ritter's gaze pauses on a large ink blotter crowned with

a statue of a black crow, its wings spread and its pointy beak raised high. It's a crude rendering that was painted long ago, and now the paint is chipping and peeling in many places. The statue looks to Ritter to be older than any other object in the room, and that's impressive enough, but what's captured his eyes are the gilded runes embossed along its base. It's a language Ritter doesn't recognize.

"That's something," he says.

"What?" Cindy asks.

Ritter frowns. "I don't know. I need Hara. He knew most every damn language ever spoken or written on this planet. But I'd lay odds that thing does something."

"Last time you said some shit like that, we ended up engulfed in Henley's playpen balls and sucked into a cave full of clown zombies."

"Zombie clowns," Moon corrects her.

"I'm not having that discussion again!" she snaps at him.

"It doesn't matter," Ritter reprimands them both. "I can't decipher it."

"Then what do we do?" Marcus asks. "Google Translate?"

They all stare at the statue atop the blotter in silence for several long moments, no one seeming able to come up with a plan.

Then, casually, Moon reaches out and grabs the statue by the crow's head, pulling it back.

A mechanical hiss issues from somewhere beneath the desktop, and Moon steps away as the entire gargantuan piece of furniture rises from the office carpet, elevating almost seven feet on long steel pistons attached to the bottom of each corner. It stops rising when a machined platform fills the hole in the floor left by the desk. A small console is bolted into the platform, a simple lever affixed to its surface.

"Holy shit, it's an elevator," Marcus says in disbelief.

All three of them stare at Moon, speechless, none more gobsmacked than Cindy.

He only shrugs. "You guys overthink shit sometimes. Everyone's seen the same movies, y'know? Even a dude like Allensworth."

Ritter claps Moon on the shoulder, though his expression remains ever passive. He motions for them all to join him on the platform beneath the desk.

Marcus racks his shotgun and Cindy unsheathes her tomahawk before following. Ritter waits until they're gathered and pulls the lever. The desk hisses at them once more and begins descending. It proves to be a short ride, as the office quickly gives way to a windowless subterranean chamber with concrete block walls and only a single, bare lightbulb dangling from the ceiling on its cord illuminating the cramped space. The lift stops as the platform beneath them touches down on the dirt floor.

"I don't like this shit," Cindy says immediately. "There ain't no way out of here. We're about to trap our damn selves."

"Wire this thing and send it back up, just in case," Ritter instructs her.

Cindy nods, quickly retrieving several items from the pockets of her tactical vest. She reaches up and begins working on the bottom of the desk.

As she does, the rest of them step off the lift, squinting into the darkness of the dimly lit space.

"It looks like an old converted fruit cellar," Ritter observes.

"That stink ain't old fruit," Cindy insists as she affixes a high-explosive device to a motion sensor and attaches both to the top of the lift.

Marcus grunts. "It's shit."

"All right!" Cindy announces, yanking the lever and stepping off the lift as it begins to rise. "We're covered."

Ritter nods, reaching up and taking hold of the cord attached to the single lightbulb.

"What's that sound?" Moon asks. "It sounds like . . . indigestion."

Ritter directs the bulb's light onto the far side of the cellar. The pale, syrupy illumination trips over a series of iron bars. A prison cell has been installed in the subterranean space.

"What the hell—" Cindy begins, and then stops, half-shocked and half-repulsed.

The cell isn't empty. Ritter casts the bulb's light on a lumpy, misshapen form covered in dull and withered scales.

"Is that . . . a demon?" Cindy asks.

"I know you," Ritter says to the cell's occupant. "You're dead."

"Many knew me," the demon says in what sounds more like rusty rakes being digested by a whale than the voice of a sentient being. "And feared me. Long ago."

"Who is he, dude?" Moon asks.

"He's the Oexial elder who choked to death on a chicken bone at Lena and Darren's first gig before he could blow the whistle on that fake angel meat," Ritter says. "This is Astaroth."

# I HAVE ALWAYS BEEN HERE

Lena isn't certain when they became the sounds of home to her, the shuffling and rattling that never fail to welcome visitors to Boosha's small corner of Sin du Jour that is equal parts apothecary, test kitchen, and arcane junk closet. Lena can't count or fully recall the number of late nights she's wandered past the always-open door to hear the ramshackle chorus of Boosha puttering around inside, attending to a dozen simultaneous and seemingly random tasks that never seem to involve organizing the room's contents, at least to the eyes of every outsider. In a chaotic environment of constantly morphing rules and circumstances, Boosha has remained an immutable constant, an anchor for Lena's work life and even, at times, her sanity.

All these thoughts tumble around Lena's mind with the occasional banging of sneakers tossed into a commercial dryer as she finds herself approaching Boosha's door after hours.

The first thing Lena sees upon entering the cramped, musty space is Boosha's gnarled blackthorn lectern. Its slanted face is hosting yet another cracked leather tome opened to wrinkled parchment pages inked with some extra-human form of language only the ageless hybrid inhabitant of these quarters has the ability to read. It was from that lectern and those crumbling old volumes that Boosha taught Lena and Darren so many lessons about Sin du Jour's eclectic clientele and the world as it really exists, so much larger and terrible and wondrous than either of the young chefs could've ever imagined.

In this room, Lena learned about goblins, the most beautiful of all God's creatures, who munch on rare gemstones for a snack, and about demons, the inhumanly spicy food–loving rival clans of hellions fighting the same generational and cultural war against one another with fire and axes that humans wage every day using social media. In this room, Lena learned about the forgotten guardians of the Earth called elementals, about centaurs and satyrs and subway trolls and a secret litany of other supernatural creatures, their history, and above all else, what they love to eat.

Boosha is hunched over a bulbous black iron pot that is half as high as she stands. Her mountain of white hair always reminds Lena of an elderly version of the Marvel Comics character Medusa. The pot sits on a lopsided wooden frame she probably hammered together herself. The gas heating element whose oil-smelling flames tickle the pot's underbelly is older than Lena and probably the last two generations of her family. A viscous concoction several shades of drab and sickly green (not unlike Boosha's skin tone) bubbles and steams inside the pot. It smells of too-sweet onions and something acrid and starchy and ashen like burnt potatoes.

Boosha is stirring the contents of the cauldron-like pot with the longest, slimmest wooden spoon Lena has ever seen. It looks like a pool cue broken in half.

"You no sleep enough," Boosha comments without preamble, ignoring Lena in favor of focusing on the syrupy goop she's sloshing around the pot.

"You never sleep," Lena points out.

Boosha grunts. "Is not the same. Sleep is food for the young. Is not food I need now."

Lena has no idea what that means, but she knows asking won't bring any clarification.

"What are you doing?" she asks instead.

"I make soup."

It occurs to Lena then that she's never actually seen Boosha eat, not really. The ancient-looking creature never joins the staff for family meal. Lena has only watched her taste test the arcane and often ancient recipes they prepare for clients of various and equally ancient species.

It further occurs to Lena how little she really knows

of the matronly hybrid at all.

"Boosha, can I ask you something?"

She scoffs. "All you do is ask."

"No, I know, but ... can I ask you something ... you know, personal?"

Boosha nods impatiently, skimming the inside walls of the pot with her spoon.

"What you are?" Lena asks, adding quickly as Boosha looks up at her with slit, offended eyes, "I mean, where do you come from?"

"Have always been here," she answers simply.

Lena's brow wrinkles. "What?"

"I have always been here," Boosha repeats, slower, as if Lena were dim or a small child. "I will always be here."

"I don't understand what that means."

Boosha's lips tighten in frustration. "Why you must understand? Do you ask these questions of grass or water or road outside?"

"I want to know," Lena says. "I feel like I should've asked a long time ago. You've taught me so much."

Boosha's pestered expression softens.

"This place," she begins, more patiently this time, "is place for teaching."

"You mean ... the buildings? Or do you mean this room?"

Boosha shrugs. "Do not know. Maybe both. I know

only this is place made to teach those who need to know. Like you, like your friend. Even Chef Bronko when he first comes here. He did not know. Is why they give him this place to cook for them. This is place made to teach."

"And you . . . you've always been here? Even before Chef Luck took over?"

Boosha nods. "I help to teach him, others who come before, others who will come after. That is all."

Lena takes a deep breath, absorbing those words. "I'd ask more, but I'm guessing what you just said, that's as much as I'll ever understand, huh?"

Boosha actually smiles at her. "You good girl. You no worry. You know what you need to know. And like I say before—"

"You'll always be here," Lena says.

Boosha nods, still smiling.

Slowly, Lena smiles back, her eyes drifting from the withered, slightly inhuman features of Boosha's face to the surface of her bubbling soup.

On impulse, Lena dips the barest tip of her right pinkie finger into the concoction and brings it to her lips, suckling it.

Her face practically implodes, and she sticks her tongue out, retching.

"That is fucking atrocious!"

Boosha hisses at her. "Language!"

"I'm sorry, but that is vile. You're going to eat that?"

"No. Is not for eating."

"Then what's it for?"

"Seeing."

"Seeing what?"

Boosha shrugs. "Whatever soup shows you."

Though she continues trying to work it out, Lena momentarily forgets about the awful taste in her mouth.

"Jett said . . . she said you knew Hara wasn't going to come back from Gluttony Bay. Is that true?"

"Knew one would not come back. Did not know who."

"But how?" Lena presses. "How did you know? The soup?"

Boosha shakes her head. "Not soup. Am made to know things. Sometimes see more than what is in books. Like Romani. Have little Romani in me."

"You have a little of *everything* in you, don't you?"

Boosha stares openly at her. "Is part of being made to know."

Lena licks her lips tentatively before asking, "Do you . . . do you know how . . . I dunno, all of this is going to end, I guess? For all of us?"

"End is always the same."

Lena sighs. "Boosha, c'mon with the riddles. You know what I mean."

"End is always the same," Boosha repeats, insistently.

"Some will die. Some will live. Some things will stop. Other things keep going. End is always the same. Do not need soup to see that."

"That's real comforting, thanks," Lena says, her sarcasm not lost even on Sin du Jour's perpetually oblivious taste tester.

"Knowing is not meant to be warm blanket," Boosha insists. "Knowing is only truth. Truth is like life, like death. They are all what is. That is all they are. You must choose what happens between."

Lena tries to laugh, but it comes out more like a moan. "What's scary is I actually think I know what you mean."

Boosha reaches up and pats her cheek with a hand that feels as soft and thin as silk.

"You will make do," she says.

Lena sighs. "So, if you don't see the end in the soup, then what *do* you see?"

Boosha dips her long wooden spoon into the murky depths and draws from the bottom of the pot, ladling what's settled in the soup atop its swampy surface. She repeats the action several times, stirring the soup in between and peering into the pot deliberately.

"I see you," Boosha pronounces.

Lena frowns. "You see me? You see me doing what?"

"Standing."

"Standing? What do you mean?"

"You are standing," Boosha confirms. "You are only one who is."

Lena's eyes darken. "Who . . . *isn't* standing, Boosha?"

The ancient woman shakes her head sadly.

"Cannot see," she declares.

Lena stares down into the pot, watching jade-tinted bubbles form and burst atop the hissing liquid.

"I never liked soup," she quietly confesses. "It's like food but not food. And that comforting feeling you get in your stomach doesn't last."

# DEMON IN A BOX

The Demon Lord Astaroth, Third of the Fallen, Tempter of Saints, who tasted the flesh of Archangel Michael in the final battle for Heaven, is taking a shit in the corner of a converted fruit cellar in a cabin in upstate New York.

"Oh, that is *rank*, dude!" Moon retches, turning away and closing his eyes.

None of them is certain which is more off-putting, the sight or the noises the decrepit demon is making.

Marcus uses the hand supporting his shotgun's slide to cover his mouth and nose. "Man, we saw some fucked-up shit in the jungle, but this just colonized all that fucked-up shit and built a fucked-up empire on top of it."

"I am certain to you I smell like death dragging week-old entrails over brimstone," the elder demon says. "I assure you, however, your ripe flesh smells even *worse* to me!"

"I'mma have to call bullshit on that," Cindy practically moans.

"I will assume this is not a rescue," Astaroth muses. "I would ask what you are doing here, but I am beyond taking even the slightest interest in human affairs."

"We were told you died," Ritter says calmly, apparently the only one able to block out the total sensory assault.

Astaroth snorts his derision. "So even my own clans-demons believed. In my captivity here, I have struggled to accept such ancient creatures could be so foolish! Our Desolate Master Himself has forgotten me, it seems."

This final admission appears to be a particular misery for the shriveled hellion, as if he's speaking of a father who never truly gave him the attention he so desperately craved.

"Even on this mortal plane, demons are made of tougher stuff, you pink, pulpy rodent."

"Then how in the hell did you end up here?" Cindy asks.

"Allensworth knew abducting me would bring the eyes and wrath of the Oexial clan and the Dark Lord Himself to his machinations. If I appeared to succumb at my age to mortal danger, however . . ."

Ritter squints in the dim light, examining the sagging, leathery folds of the elder demon's lumpy, misshapen form. Even amidst the many lines of age and millennia-old battle scars, he can make out fresh wounds.

Ritter frowns. "He's been torturing you, hasn't he? Allensworth?"

"How can you tell?" Marcus asks.

Astaroth snorts again. "'Torture.' What humans call torture, demons know as pleasure."

"Like in *Hellraiser*?" Moon asks.

Even Astaroth ignores that question

"What did he to want to know?" Ritter asks.

"All the secrets of Hell."

The foursome waits to hear more.

" . . . Can you be a little more specific?" Marcus presses when no more information is offered.

"He wanted intel on the Oexial clan," Ritter says, the situation beginning to uncloud for him. "He wanted to know where Hell is vulnerable, in our world and theirs. He's setting your clan up for the Vig'nerash, isn't he? He's helping them take over."

Astaroth stares at him through the bars, the surprise in his reaction more evident in his silence than the demon's puckered face.

"That's what Gluttony Bay was all about," Ritter continues, and it's clear he's working it out for himself as much as the rest of them. "It's why it was filled with Vig'nerash demons. He's been sucking up to them for decades. They're trading coups, aren't they? Allensworth is helping the Vig'nerash unseat the Oexial and take over Hell so they'll back him taking over the Sceadu and everything that's left on Earth. He wants to run it all."

Even Moon, never the most introspective or self-aware among them, is livid. "Jesus, that's some Bond villain–type shit."

Ritter shakes his head, lost in his own dark self-realization. "Allensworth. He planned the whole fucking thing," he says bitterly, sounding angrier at himself than Allensworth. "Even before Consoné, he set us up. The angel, the demon clan banquet, Wrinkles in the cell here choking to death in front of everyone so Allensworth could hijack him without anyone knowing—"

"I will vomit in your soul, human," Astaroth spits at him.

"—it was all smoke. We've always been his weapons. *I've* always been his weapon."

"Not the time or place to get all in your feelings, my dude," Cindy says.

Marcus nods. "Soul-search later, bro. We're on the clock."

"This is what we needed," Cindy reminds him. "This is what Bronko sent us here to get. This is our *proof*. We take Cobra Commander here's ass to the Sceadu, he spills the ugly beans, and they take out Allensworth before he launches his endgame. Mission accomplished."

Astaroth laughs. It's a shrill and awful rasping that would be a death spasm coming from a human being.

"What's so funny, Pappy O'Lumps?" Cindy asks the demon.

"The human you know as 'Allensworth' is only one of many who have borne the name. I knew the first of them as Ahns'w'rk not long after you muck-dwelling vermin finally mastered fire. It is a mantle taken on by those of your kind who walk between worlds, bridging the unearthly and earthly planes, brokering life and death between humans and the higher creatures of existence. The title attracts the most craven among you, those who above all else yearn for power beyond paltry wealth or empty political authority. *This* Allensworth, however, is the most virulently ambitious yet. He is willing to upset the balance of Hell to rule on your Earth. Your tiny, insignificant rabble has no *hope* of unseating his plans."

Cindy's eyes narrow in cold resolution. "We'll see about that shit. Help me get these bars open and let's bounce."

She reaches down to unlatch her tactical tomahawk.

"Well played," Luciana congratulates them. "You have achieved your apparent objective."

The spirit has reappeared. She's standing serenely behind the assemblage in the cellar, spectral hands delicately folded in front of her spectral body, unaffected smile ever present.

They all turn to face her.

"I guess that Polaroid juju wore off," Marcus says to Ritter.

"Eat me," he quietly and passively rejoins.

"Unfortunately," Luciana adds, ignoring their banter, "you are all going to be flayed alive."

The pounding of several dozen heavy boots on the cabin floor begins to thump directly over the foursome's heads. Most of them look up to watch the plaster being shaken loose by the quaking.

Ritter's gaze, however, remains affixed on Luciana.

"It's amazing how far behind current events you can fall, being out of action just a few minutes," he says to the spirit.

Her smile falters, and Luciana cocks her head just so, her eyes asking the human what he knows that she doesn't.

They can all hear those heavy boots surrounding the desk in Allensworth's private office.

"Hit the deck!" Cindy hollers, dropping to the cellar floor and covering her head with her arms.

Ritter, Marcus, and Moon heed her warning, their bodies flattening to the floor as if gravity in the confined space has quadrupled.

Even Astaroth shrinks into the foul, shit-smelling recesses of his cell.

Luciana stares up at the outline in the ceiling of the hidden desk lift, the beginnings of realization touching the edges of her eyes.

In the next moment, they widen behind her oversized glasses.

They hear the sound of the secret elevator being activated. The ceiling at first muffles the report of the explosion that follows, then a balcony-sized section collapses into the cellar, tearing the lift frame from its moorings. Allensworth's massive onyx slab desk crashes through the sudden hole and pulverizes the concrete floor of the cellar, raising a cloud of dusk that conceals the flying shrapnel. The desk's wooden frame has been reduced to charred splinters.

A severed human arm wearing a tactical glove and the sleeve of a flak jacket is still attached to the onyx desktop.

Luciana sighs in irritation, physically unaffected by the blast and its aftermath in every way.

Ritter and the others are temporarily choking on the dust and shaking shrapnel from their hair and clothes. Their eardrums would be blown out right now if it weren't for their sacred wax plugs. As it is, every human head in the cellar is buzzing and filled with throbbing pain. Ritter is the first to make it back to his feet, followed by Cindy, who hauls Moon off the floor none too gently while Ritter offers his brother a hand.

Behind the iron bars of his cage, Astaroth is cursing them all out in his shrill demon-speak.

"That bought us some time!" Cindy shouts at Ritter

through bouts of hacking coughs. "We need to get Uncle Happy out of this cage and to Consoné and the Sceadu!"

Luciana makes a *tsk-tsk* sound with her tongue, shaking her head sorrowfully.

"I'm afraid we can't have that," she says.

The shotgun in Marcus's hand swings away from his body, pulling itself free of his grip, hovering several feet from the cellar floor.

"What the fuck?" he yells in surprise.

Before any of them can react further, the muzzle angles between the bars of Astaroth's cell and an invisible finger squeezes the trigger.

The burst-fruit sound of his withered, scaly skull exploding is lost beneath the thunder of the shotgun's report.

"Fuck!" Ritter shouts in an uncharacteristic display of emotion, particularly anger.

The shotgun spins in place, stopping when its wide bore is level with Ritter's neck. Its heavy slide ratchets back, discharging the spent shell that just decapitated Astaroth to make room for a fresh round of mayhem.

Cindy's eyes widen and she screams, "No!"

The trigger of the shotgun pulls back.

Ritter closes his eyes.

A hollow metallic *snap* echoes throughout the cellar.

The rest is silence that lasts several excruciating moments. Ritter's eyes open and he stares into the darkness of the shotgun barrel, his expression still utterly blank.

The weapon is empty.

"Holy shit, dude," Moon mutters amidst his entire body exhaling in relief.

Luciana's smile contorts into the thinnest frown.

"Well," she says stiffly. "That is a shame."

As they all look on, the animating force controlling the shotgun releases its hold and the weapon falls to the cellar floor, clattering loudly before collapsing onto its side.

"You fake-ass phantasmal *bitch*!" Cindy curses her, enraged, turning on the meticulously groomed specter.

Before Luciana can summon a saccharine and vitriolic retort, Ritter palms a simple boot flask and spins the cap loose with the edge of his thumb. He flicks it at the specter like a sanctifying priest. The strip of water that sails through her illusory form leaves behind a slash of white light across her canary-yellow suit jacket. That light quickly begins spreading through the rest of the apparition's torso.

Luciana looks down at the infectious radiance, then at Ritter. She frowns as it begins seeping up her neck and engulfing her face.

"That was very rude," she chastises him just before her entire form is swallowed and dispersed by white light that fades just as quickly.

113

Cindy watches Luciana disappear with murder in her eyes. She turns around and takes hold of Ritter's wrist, raising the flask in his hand to her face and sniffing the rim.

"That ain't holy water," she says.

Ritter shrugs. "Whiskey barreled by monks. Sacramental by default. It works in a pinch."

Marcus snatches up his shotgun. "We still need to get out of here and we can't go back the way they came. That blast won't have taken them all out."

"I got this," Moon says, apparently trying to sound like an action star in a big-budget summer blockbuster.

Cindy side-eyes him. "What do you mean, you 'got this?'"

Without answering her, Moon reaches down the collar of the *Schlock Mercenary* T-shirt he's wearing beneath his jacket and pulls out a chartreuse gemstone set inside obsidian jaws and hung from a thick gold chain. He paces quickly to the far wall of the cellar. Each concrete block mortared there is almost the size of Moon's torso, and twice as thick.

Cindy watches him dubiously, looking over at Ritter with the same emotion plastered all over her face.

Ritter only shrugs, seeming more curious that concerned.

"Whatever you're gonna do, do it now, Dazed and

Confused!" Marcus shouts after Moon, racking his shotgun and pointing it at the still-smoking hole in the ceiling.

"Fuck, you're old," Moon fires back at him.

He presses the gemstone against the center of the cellar wall. It scrapes there, gently, like glass upon broken teeth. Moon brings his wrist to his mouth and uses his teeth to peel back the sleeve of his jacket. Scrawled messily along the inside of his forearm is what appears to the rest of them to be words in some arcane language spelled out phonetically and utilizing an obscene amount of hyphens.

"Shit," Moon mutters as his eyes quickly scan the words. "Wrong one."

He quickly shakes his sleeve back down his arm and uses that hand to pull up his right pant leg almost to the knee. More phonetic crib notes are jotted in red Sharpie down his calf.

"Ah-hah!" he proclaims triumphantly.

Moon lifts and bends his knee, angling the bottom of his right leg awkwardly and crooking his neck at the same time to clearly see the words.

He begins reciting the inscription under his breath. It sounds like unintelligible muttering to the rest of them, but as he does, the edges of the gemstone pressed against the wall begin to emit an eerie green light. Ritter and the others squint as they all question perceiving what appears to be a slight, shimmering wave ripple through the seemingly solid face of the wall.

When Moon pushes his free hand against the wall, his fingers disappear through it as if the concrete were mud, eventually immersing his arm to the elbow.

"Nuh-uh," Cindy half-marvels, half-outright doubts. "I am *not* believing this."

She jogs over to the wall and swipes a finger at what is now an incredibly malleable surface, coming away with a clumpy smear of some creamy substance. She sniffs at it experimentally with her brow furrowed and finally tastes the miraculously transformed emulsion with the barest tip of her tongue.

Cindy's eyes widen. "Is this shit . . . *meringue*?"

Moon nods. "Raspberry, should be."

"I hear shuffling!" Marcus warns the rest of them. "They're recovering up there!"

"What about the subterranean soil, Moon?" Ritter asks.

Moon stares at him blankly. "Huh?"

"The dirt on the other side of the wall, boy!" Cindy shouts impatiently and loud enough in his ear to make Moon jump.

"Oh! Yeah, right, no, it . . . *should* go all the way to the top, and it's thick enough we can, like, burrow through it.

Y'know, like moles or whatever."

Ritter doesn't quite frown, but his always-serious expression darkens just a bit.

"Even if it does go all the way up," Cindy says, "how do we breathe whilst we burrow?"

A shotgun blast answers her, Marcus racking the slide and discharging the hollowed shell as he backpedals toward the wall of raspberry meringue.

"I am legendary for how long I can hold my breath," he informs her as he brushes past Cindy, flashing a grin at her.

Marcus briefly tests the viscosity of the wall with the butt of his shotgun. Satisfied, he glances back at Cindy and yells before diving headfirst into the meringue, "*Legendary!*"

Moon looks at Ritter. "That was a joke about going down on her, right?"

"*Yes, dammit*, of course it was!" Cindy angrily shouts at him, shoving Moon aside.

She inhales deeply and holds it, dislodging a giant glob of raspberry meringue and splattering the cellar floor with it as she pulls herself into the wall.

The sound of heavy boots and smoke-strangled voices shouting begins to surround the hole in the cellar roof.

"I did good, right?" Moon hurriedly asks Ritter as he shrugs off his cream-stained coat.

"Moon, if we're all still alive in five minutes? *Then* you did good."

With that, Ritter takes one handful of Moon's comic-strip T-shirt and another handful of his belt and hurls him like a hay bale into the raspberry meringue.

# HEADS, YOU LOSE

Bronko hasn't been home to his Manhattan brownstone in almost two weeks. It's easy enough living out of Sin du Jour, considering the size of the compound-like series of brick buildings and their seemingly endless facilities; it's certainly not a place you'd ever go hungry. But lacking fresh clothing, not to mention a moment alone, Bronko decides it's time to pay a quick visit and at least read his mail.

His cell phone rings as he sits in the back of an honest-to-goodness taxicab (Bronko does *not* hold with the Ubers and Lyfts of modern society). He answers it and his blood runs cold as he listens to Ritter explain what happened in Allensworth's cabin, every gory, unfulfilled detail. For Bronko, it's not unlike having a loved one on their deathbed and finally receiving the terrible news you've been expecting yet not wanting to hear.

"There's nothin' to be done, then," he finally says when Ritter has finished spinning the tale. "I'm glad y'all are whole. We'll take comfort in that, if nothin' else. Hightail it back home now."

Bronko ends the call and stashes his phone, a swarm of bees seeming to be buzzing between his ears. The rest of his body feels numb.

He disembarks from the cab in the middle of the afternoon. The street is quiet and his door appears undisturbed as Bronko approaches the stoop. Halfway up the steps, however, Bronko pauses, at first confused, and then concerned.

There's a giant present awaiting him on his doorstep.

"Hard to believe this ends well," he mutters.

The box is large enough to hold two Crock-Pots and is elaborately gift-wrapped with gold paper and silver ribbons. The embossed tag has the word "Byron" etched in elegant lettering with nothing else written on it.

Bronko walks slowly up the remaining steps and kneels down slowly while cursing the unnatural symphony of creaks and pops issuing from his knees. He scrutinizes the box without touching it, the old bomb cliché running through his mind, followed by a montage of far more gruesome, inhuman possibilities for what might await him inside the box should the sender be less than an admirer of his.

He realizes he's only postponing the inevitable and leans over the box. Shaking the lid free, he sets it aside and peers within.

Bronko immediately looks away, shutting his eyes

tight as he coughs several times. The smell is already firmly ensconced in both of his nostrils, however. He's uncertain whether it's that olfactory assault causing his guts to churn, or whether the sight of what's inside the box that's causing that particular sensation. He's less confused about the source of the sheer dread that is slowly spreading through his entire body.

He doesn't have to look inside the box to examine its contents; a split-second viewing of them has burned the image in graphic detail into his brain. Bronko looks again anyway, if for no other reason than to verify his tired, frightened mind isn't lying to him.

Two heads, human heads, have been carefully placed inside the large box. There's no blood; the stumps of their surgically severed necks have been carefully cauterized.

One of the heads belongs to the new Allensworth.

The other head belongs to Enzo Consoné, newly elected President of the Sceadu, the shadow government of the supernatural world.

The dread completely takes hold of Bronko. The implications of these savage tokens are enough to spin the world around him until he's afraid he'll vomit into the box.

Not only is Allensworth, *his* Allensworth, alive and well, he's forgone the clandestine usurping for which he attempted to subvert Sin du Jour time and time again.

These severed heads must be the result of a full-on palace coup. He's assassinated Consoné and gone so far as to attack his own former allies in the shadowy, nameless agency that oversees human-supernatural diplomatic relations. He's taken out anyone who would oppose him.

Bronko can scarcely breathe as he notices an object has been carefully wedged between the cold blue lips of Enzo Consoné's decapitated head. With trembling fingers, Bronko gently pries what turns out to be a folded piece of paper from the dead man's mouth. The tremors only intensify as he hastily unwraps its edges.

It's a simple note, unsigned, short and to the point.

*I'll see you all soon, Byron.*

Bronko lets the slip of paper flit from his fingertips and back into the box. He stands, very slowly, not trusting his legs. Once he has his feet back underneath him, Bronko stares out over the serenity of the leaf-littered street in front of his brownstone. There are no dark vans or suspicious cars with tinted windows parked at the curb. There are no errant dog-walkers who might be spying on him from afar. It's the same street it's always been.

Of course it is. Why wouldn't it be? Allensworth wouldn't leave a package like this on his doorstep just to murder him a moment later. He wants Bronko to live with the anticipation for at least a little while.

For some reason, it's that thought which sobers him,

reconnecting Bronko with the head chef who gives the orders and has for as long as he can remember.

Bronko draws in a slow, deep, cleansing breath, flexing his fingers and balling them into fists several times to bring his trembling under control.

"Here we go, then," he says. "War it is."

# PART II

# WAR IN THREE COURSES: SERVED COLD

# MORE GOOD THAN HARM

James fills a Dixie cup with a finger of Swedish brandy and raises the paper rim to Darren's lips, cooing to him gently as he drinks.

"There you are, mon amour. This is, how they say, good for what ails you. You will be right in no time."

Darren swallows hard, the alcohol warming his ragged throat in a soothing way rather than stinging, as he would've expected.

"Thank you," he whispers.

They're sitting on the worn leather sofa in Bronko's office, a plush blanket wrapped around Darren's shoulders. James has prepared a bowl of stew for him that Darren has yet to touch.

"I wish that we could go home," James laments. "I would like to be in our own bed tonight. Chef says it is too dangerous now."

"I believe it."

James places his hand behind Darren's head gently and kisses his temple.

"We will find our way through this," he whispers. "I

promise you, mon amour."

Darren closes his eyes and rests his forehead against James's bald scalp.

"You're too good for this world," he says. "I used to think of myself that way, but I wasn't good; I was just . . . naive. I know you've seen bad shit, but you're still good."

"It is because of the things I have seen that I know how important it is to be your best self."

Darren smiles, almost ruefully. "See? Only a ridiculously good person would say crap like that."

"Is this a bad time?"

Ritter is standing in the open doorway, watching them without expression.

James and Darren look up at him, James quickly turning his gaze to Darren in concern.

Darren, however, appears undisturbed by Ritter's presence.

"Do we have any other kinds of times lately?"

Ritter nods. "Fair. I want to ask you how you're feeling, but I want to make it clear I just mean physically. I know how stupid a question that is to apply to any other part of you right now."

"Physically? I feel like I have the worst hangover ever."

"Good. That'll pass."

"What do you need, Ritter?" James asks hastily, seeming less upset with Ritter and more worried about how he might upset Darren.

Ritter hangs his head, silent at first. When he looks back at Darren, his expression is strained, as if he's barely containing the emotion he feels.

"Look, you trusted me and I fucked you. There's no other way to say it."

Darren nods. "Lena told me what happened. She told me about your brother. She didn't say it like she's forgiven you, though."

"I don't expect her to. I don't expect you to, either."

"But you're sorry?" Darren asks.

"I am. More than I can ever say, and more than I can ever make up for."

"Well." Darren looks at James, who looks back. They both smile. "I'm alive and I didn't kill anybody. In the long run, I'm going to choose to believe you did me more good than harm."

Ritter swallows. "I wish I could believe that, kid."

Darren stares up at him intently. He suddenly looks far older.

"You did a shitty thing, but you didn't make me do anything, okay? I gave in to . . . whatever that was. I know that now. I could've told it to fuck off. It was a choice. It just played on everything I always hated about myself, and everything I was afraid of. And I couldn't see it. I do now. That part is on me."

"Well, you were strong enough to break free," Ritter says.

"Barely."

Ritter fixes him with hard, knowing eyes. "*Barely* is enough."

Darren almost seems comforted by that, but the pain and the memories are still too fresh.

"What about you and Lena?" he asks, intentionally changing the subject.

Ritter shrugs. "We're treating it like the end of the world, I guess. Because it just might be. And if the world's ending, a lot of the petty shit just isn't important any more."

Darren nods. "Okay. Well, if it's the end of the world, let's have a drink. James has this kick-ass brandy."

James raises the bottle helpfully, smiling.

For the first time, Ritter looks something close to relieved.

"A drink sounds like a good idea," he says.

# SHORTHANDED

Thoughts of revenge are the only thing currently distracting Allensworth from the agony of half his body parts slowly becoming new body parts.

Watching Sircus, the warrior-chieftain of the Vig'nerash demon clan, preen in front of several mirrors while harpy attendants affix armor composed of the bones of his enemies to his leathery hide does little to salve the pain or block out the crackling sound of Allensworth's skin hardening and his bones reshaping. Even the otherworldly herbs Sircus's surgeon gave him to ingest seem to barely dull the sensation of knives piercing half his nerve endings.

They are dozens of yards beneath Wall Street, where the Vig'nerash warriors are massing around several open hellmouths that serve as portals to the underworld (90 percent of New York City hellmouths are located under Wall Street, for obvious reasons). They're preparing for the second phase of Allensworth's plan, the full-scale assault on Hell itself.

Allensworth finds he couldn't care less about this part.

There's only one thing on his mind, the desire that's been steadily gnawing his innards with greater and greater ferocity since Gluttony Bay.

"I can almost *feel* your impatience," Sircus idly remarks. "And I have always known you to be such a calm and calculating being."

"I've undergone some drastic changes as of late."

"Necessary changes," Sircus reminds him.

"I am aware," Allensworth says through tense lips. "It's the *cause* of those necessary changes that requires my immediate attention."

"If slaughtering those cooks was such a priority, you should have done it before you staged your little coup and committed us to open conflict."

"I *had* to escalate the timetable after they violated my private home and that bastard Astaroth told them everything! Besides, I wanted them to know what's coming."

"And now?"

"I want what's coming to arrive."

"It will. *After* my warriors crush the Oexial clan here and in Hell, and I sit atop the Throne of the Fallen, as you promised."

"I've fulfilled my commitments. I've isolated the Oexial for you. They have no support, no allies, above or below. The Dark Lord Himself couldn't get a phone call returned from Los Angeles to New York right now.

They will never *be* more vulnerable."

"Then you have only to wait until we sweep them all into the abyss."

"I am sick of waiting!" Allensworth says frothily.

"My legions aren't your private army, Allensworth! The Vig'nerash have waited ages to unseat the Oexial, and those old fossils will fight to the last demon."

"One battalion for two hours is all I would require," Allensworth insists. "We'd crush Sin du Jour and your warriors would be back in time to taste fresh Oexial entrails."

Sircus sighs, and it sounds more like a snake hissing. "I will spare what warriors I can, *when* I can. If you wish to exact your vengeance sooner, then you will simply have to use your own forces."

"What forces are those? The Sceadu is headless and decimated. Regular government resources are scattered. Most of them don't know who is in charge right now. It will take weeks to consolidate them, at least."

Sircus dismisses his attendants with a wave of his talons and turns to regard Allensworth.

"Are you telling me a human of your associations and influence cannot summon enough favors to create a makeshift force sufficient to lay siege to a catering company?"

The question seems to sober Allensworth. He stares up at the demon clan leader with a renewed energy in his mismatched expression.

Slowly, a sinister grin spreads through the still-human half of his mouth.

"I suppose I can make a few calls," he says.

# FAMILY MEAL

Usually, it's a single-dish affair, Bronko cooking up a huge pot of paella on Monday with Friday's seafood or smoking a batch of pulled pork and tossing it in a tangy house-made barbeque sauce highlighted by a reduction of Mexican Coca-Cola (all the while loudly and virulently cursing the high-fructose corn syrup industry). Sometimes, he'll serve the succulent shredded pork on Hawaiian roll sliders topped by scorching-hot pickles brined by Bronko himself in a sixty-year-old barrel into which he tosses flayed habaneros and ghost peppers, seeds and all, and drips the extract of Carolina Reapers imported directly from Rock Hill.

When Dorsky cooks for family meal, he always tries to elevate the spread (including wanting to sous-vide *everything* after watching Bradley Cooper in the movie *Burnt*, or more precisely wanting to *be* Bradley Cooper in the movie *Burnt*), but the practical demands of feeding an entire kitchen staff on a busy workday usually reins in his perpetually overachieving, ceaselessly-trying-to-be-Bronko nature. Still, his five-cheese raviolis in brown butter with jalapeño and mint pesto have been a longtime favorite of the line.

The family meals prepared by Lena usually see her resurrect the Hungarian comfort dishes of her childhood, stuffing cabbage with a peppery mix of beef and pork and onions and bacon, simmering a hot and spicy fisherman's soup, or stewing a meat-and-vegetable goulash. In a way, these dishes exemplify Lena's cooking far more than the fine-dining fare she prepares for Sin du Jour's clients: simple, clean, flawlessly executed, and not meant to prove anything to anyone except herself.

Tonight is a different affair. Tonight's family meal at Sin du Jour is a potlatch spectacle stamped with every staff member's fingerprint, attending by everyone save Boosha, forever tethered to her tiny ramshackle apothecary. They've all prepared their best dishes, or rather the dishes they'd most want to share with the people closest to them. For the line cooks, it's a showcase, an inverse last meal, one dish by which to be remembered and leave their mark on the kitchen.

James has re-created the cheeseburger that was his first meal in America, from a stand near Grand Central Station, overloaded with caramelized onions and butter pickles. Chevet spent three days marinating chicken in wine from his family's vineyard for a timeless coq au vin. Tenryu has transformed the aborted cheese that is tofu into something sumptuous and texturally pleasing using crab sauce and real wasabi (it's highly likely all the wasabi you've ever eaten is dyed horseradish). Rollo's scratch-made miniature cheese blintzes are exquisitely delicate and surprisingly light, everything the gruff Eastern European bear of a man is not.

Lena has crafted a perfectly clear consommé of such deep and evolving flavor, it's like tasting some sort of magic trick. None of them, including Bronko, are able to deduce how she developed that kind of flavor in such a simple and transparent dish.

"I'll tell ya, Tarr," the executive chef says after letting his last spoonful of the consommé slide down his throat. "You could give me this alongside a plate of Kobe beef and million-dollar truffles stacked into a perfect tower, and this here soup is what I'd remember."

It's the most meaningful compliment Lena has ever received.

Sin du Jour's non-kitchen staff has gotten in on the act as well. Cindy offers up a rendition of her favorite Mediterranean dish from her favorite Mediterranean restaurant, bacon-wrapped dates stuffed with chorizo and served with a piquillo pepper sauce. Even White Horse managed a Crock-Pot full of tough, chewy goat (he claims his people prefer the consistency of the meat that way and always have).

After an hour of passing every dish around the table several times and sharing the kind of talk that isn't small yet intentionally avoids the larger issues at hand in favor of frivolity and mostly bad jokes, Bronko stands at the head of the long buffet table around which they're all seated.

The chatter quiets. The rattling of glasses and silverware dies down.

"It's not my aim to stand up here and make a speech," he begins.

"Sure it is, Chef."

"Shut up, Tag," Bronko instructs his sous chef, eliciting laughter from the rest of them, even Nikki, who swats Dorsky as a form of reprimand.

Bronko takes a deep breath. "I just wanted to cook. Y'know? I wasn't more'n a li'l ol' hick from Beeville, Texas, just another meathead who washed out as a pro football player. I didn't have shit else. But my mama taught me how to cook, and I was good at it. People liked my food. They liked me in the kitchen. I could make myself heard through my cooking. At the start, that was all I wanted. It purely was. Then came the money and the agents and managers and producers and . . . I just let myself get swallowed up by all of it. I stopped paying the right kind of attention to my life. I ignored my way through two busted marriages. Got to the point I didn't have a 'friend' didn't work for me or make money off me some way. And when I hit the skids, there wasn't a soul among them stuck around to see the crash. I did every damn thing wrong a body could do in my position, and it landed me in the worst spot. . . ."

Bronko's words fade into memories only he can see. He shakes them away like errant water drops from his temples.

"I ended up here. It was my last-chance saloon, that's all. I hated it at first. I purely did. It felt like a jail. I didn't wanna end up here, ya understand. But I surely am glad I did. Because y'all are the only—"

He breaks then, his voice gone hoarse and tears prickling the corners of his eyes.

"Y'all are the only family I ever had, and I wish like hell I'd been smart enough to lead you somewhere better, anywhere but here. I'm so sorry, y'all."

By the time he's finished, Bronko is weeping silently.

Nikki is quick to stand up from her seat and wrap her arms around him, or at least attempt to encircle his massive frame. Bronko holds her like a cherished daughter.

"None of us are here because we have to be, Chef," she assures him. "We're here because we want to be, because this is where we belong."

"She's right, Chef," Lena adds.

That sentiment emanating from her is enough to

shock Bronko's tears into abatement. He stares at her over the top of Nikki's perfectly formed victory rolls, the reddened eyes behind their glassy sheen watching her curiously.

"We belong here," Lena confirms. "All of us."

That seems to satisfy Bronko on a level he can't even vocalize, or at least he doesn't try. Choking back whatever tears remain, he pats Nikki on the back, and the two of them return to their seats.

"Thanks, y'all," he says to the table.

Each of them raises whatever glasses they have without any of them being told to do so. It just seems to feel right to everyone gathered there.

"To the Chef!" Dorsky toasts.

The sentiment is echoed by each of them before they all drink.

"Is it time for dessert?" Pacific asks in the wake of the toast. "Because that's where I've planted my flag."

He removes a package from his coat protected by crumpled aluminum foil and begins unwrapping it.

"I smell fudge!" Nikki proclaims. "Are those brownies?"

"Homemade with the secret ingredient," Pacific confirms, passing the unwrapped package of dark, hastily cut squares to his right.

"THC?" Cindy asks.

"Love, brah," Pacific assures her. "Love."

Examining one of the homemade confections, Bronko glowers down the table at Pacific. "Pac, no bullshit now, boy. Are these pot brownies?"

Pacific's perpetually mellow demeanor melts into something uncharacteristically somber. "I don't want to lie to you, boss," he says, equally solemn. "So I won't. I'll tell you the straight truth. . . . I do *not* remember."

Everyone laughs, Bronko loudest of all.

The moment doesn't last, or at least it has lasted as long as it can. There's an electric sizzle above the center of the table, and Droopy Hound appears there in a flicker of static and animated color. His sagging, defeated jowls are hanging from a dark hood. The demonic cartoon is clad as the Grim Reaper, complete with comically crooked scythe.

"They're coming," he announces in his dreary monotone voice without preamble.

Bronko stands so quickly, his chair is skidded back five feet.

"What's coming?" he demands.

"Allensworth, sir," Droopy Hound explains. "He's leading a procession of vehicles up Forty-third Avenue right now. They're coming."

Nikki's hands involuntarily cover her mouth. "Oh, my God."

Ritter and the rest of his team stand, reacting with military poise and efficiency.

"How long?" Cindy asks the toon.

"Perhaps fifteen minutes, ma'am. The streets appear to have been cleared for miles."

"Fuck!" Marcus curses. "I thought we'd have more warning."

"I did my best, sir," Droopy Hound insists, though his trademark tone never falters.

"We don't have time to rally the troops," Ritter says to Bronko.

"Call 'em anyway," Bronko instructs him. "All of 'em, anyone who'll come. If they get here in time, they'll be a help to whoever's left. If not, it won't matter."

The weight of those words stuns and quiets most of them, all except Ritter, Cindy, and Marcus, who spring into action, Moon eventually following on their heels.

"Y'all know what to do," Bronko says to the rest of them. "It's battle stations. We went over this as best we could. Just do your jobs. That's all I ever asked of any of you."

White Horse abruptly stands, licking fudge from his fingertips. "How about I buy y'all some time? Give the cavalry a chance to get here? Not my favorite analogy, ya understand, but under the circumstances—"

"What are you talking about, Pop?" Little Dove asks,

the initial shock on her face transformed into concern.

"I'm going to go out there and meet them," he calmly informs her. "Good ol'-fashioned guerilla tactic. I'll hold 'em up as long as I can. Hit-and-run, like."

"That's not part of the plan, White Horse," Bronko says.

"Neither was them showing up on our doorstep with no time to get situated or call in reinforcements."

"They'll kill you!" Little Dove shouts at him.

"That's a lot of artillery coming our way," Bronko reminds him. "What can you honestly do against that all by yourself?"

"More'n you know, white man," White Horse says with a grin and a wink. "Besides, my people have a saying. When you see the rattlesnake poised to strike, strike first."

"You just made that up!" Little Dove protests.

"I read it on the Internet!" White Horse insists.

"This isn't a game, Pop!"

White Horse sighs, his tone lowering rather than rising. "I know that. Listen to me now. We all have to deal with our destiny. I've put mine off longer'n anyone I know. I've helped you to the foothills of yours. You have to walk the rest of the way up that hill alone, whether I'm around or not. Tonight's the night I finally face up to what I've been runnin' from all these years."

Tears are spilling down Little Dove's cheeks as she pleads with him. "I can't lose you, too."

White Horse reaches up and cups her cheek in his hand, the rough edge of his thumb smoothing away the salty stains there.

"I'm an old man," he says, sounding as sincere and worldly as she's ever heard him sound. "This is what happens, if we're lucky. You have a whole family here. You're not alone. I owe you so damn much, for everything I didn't do and everything you did do for me, especially these past few months. You brought me back from the dead. There's nothin' those bastards can do to me. I only need one thing from this world now, and that's for you to keep going, to live. If you can do that, it doesn't matter what happens when I walk out there, y'hear?"

His words do nothing to stem the flow of her tears, but Little Dove doesn't protest further. Instead, she steps forward and clings to him, hard, burying her face in the denim of his jacket, reveling in the smell of tobacco and weed and a thousand nights at the racetrack that usually repels her.

White Horse holds her close and kisses the top of her head. "I live as long as you live," he whispers to her. "You'll always find me in the Fourth World. I've taught you how."

Little Dove nods against his chest, sucking air as she

attempts to regain control of her emotions.

He carefully disengages her and steps back, offering his granddaughter a final, warm smile as he gently grips her arms.

No one else speaks as White Horse turns around and walks away from them, his wearied gait carrying him like a broken-down gunfighter swaggering off to meet one final challenge.

"Maybe," Bronko whispers to himself as the old medicine man disappears from sight. "Maybe we got a shot."

# AS ELOQUENT AS A RATTLESNAKE'S TAIL

They're rolling up Forty-third Avenue, a procession of half a dozen armored, matte-black vehicles. Most of them are troop carriers, squat and ugly conveyances with bulging steel plates designed to pack in as many soldiers as possible for safe delivery to the battlefield. The lead vehicle, however, is the kind a SWAT team would use to take down entire walls. It's a six-ton tank with a fourteen-foot battering ram instead of a barrel. The manhole cover–sized steel plate on the end of the ram has been scrawled with the words WON'T YOU BE MY NEIGHBOR?

White Horse walks up the center line of an eerily deserted Long Island City street. The only sound that can be heard for blocks in every direction is the hard soles of his boots clacking against the pavement. He wonders if they cleared these streets using mystical means, or whether they did what their kind has been doing in this country ever since enough of them piled off a leaky, shit-smelling boat: bully people from their path, destroying anything that could not or refused to move. Neither means would surprise him.

He stops walking when he reaches the middle of the intersection of Forty-third Avenue and Twenty-first Street. White Horse expected his sour guts to be churning like butter mixed with gasoline by now; for all his bold words and courageous sentiment back at the dinner table, he was actually terrified down to his core. A large part of him, the aspect of indifference and cynicism and borderline nihilism he'd spent many decades perfecting, balked as he'd stood up to proclaim he'd head the enemy off at the pass. That part shrieked a torrent of curses so vile, he didn't know he retained those words and phrases in his brain.

In this moment, however, he feels only a warm sense of calm, something almost serene in its composure.

As the battering ram approaches Twenty-first Street, White Horse wonders if they'll attempt to simply roll over him, or even veer and ignore the lone, withered figure barring their path. He begins summoning that thing deep inside him, the portal he was born with that allowed him to call between worlds, to speak to what has gone beyond and seek its aid and wisdom (although, facing the perpetual twilight, White Horse suddenly wishes he'd spent more time harnessing that wisdom and less time simply demanding aid for his own purposes).

To his surprise, when the battering ram enters the intersection, the hulking machine grinds to a stop, the rest of the procession halting behind it. The end of the ram is close enough for White Horse to see the chips in the painted letters.

"I am White Horse!" he cries at the armored monstrosity. "The Earth sung its deepest secrets to my people while yours were cornholing goats and speaking in low grunts! And you're standing between me and my last chance not to fuck everything up! That's a bad place to be!"

In response, the top hatch of the vehicle springs open and a partially cloaked head peers above it. White Horse can only see half the man's face in the night, but he recognizes Allensworth from his many visits to Sin du Jour, especially that phony pitchman's smile the man always wears.

"Good evening, Mr. White Horse! It's lovely to see you again. Are you just out for an evening missive? That's a good thing for a man of your advanced years. I'm afraid your route is poorly chosen, however. Would you mind repairing yourself to the sidewalk?"

"You should turn back, white man," the old Hatałii warns him. "You won't like how this all ends."

"Oh, but I will. This is the part I'm going to enjoy the most. This is all just for me. Yes, after the bother you've all caused me, tonight is like my birthday and Christmas all rolled up in one fine Turkish rug."

White Horse nods, his eyes falling on Allensworth like raining shrapnel. "So be it."

"I must admit, I am genuinely curious how precisely you imagine spirit magic will aid you in this situation. But perhaps that's why your people stumbled when they found themselves beset by armored and mounted soldiers in the first place."

"If you can't figure out how the spirits of a million pissed-off Navajo might come in handy in a fight like this, then you've never *been* in a fight like this, you steaming pile of elk shit."

Though he seems unperturbed, the smile never vacating his lips, Allensworth is silent for a prolonged moment.

Finally, he says, "I'm going to run you over now. I've enjoyed our chat."

When White Horse raises his arms and opens his mouth, the voice that booms from it causes the very air to shake. Thunder cracks on the heel of his words and lightning seems to flash through the very street.

It's enough to cause Allensworth to tilt back, startled. He quickly dips his head back inside the tank and pulls the hatch shut.

White Horse grins. In that moment, he feels like a young man.

In that moment, he feels born anew with a clean slate stretching before him forever.

He also knows forever won't last very long at all.

# THE WAITING ROOM

The lobby is the natural front line in any attack on Sin du Jour, so naturally that's where Ritter, Marcus, and Cindy have been stationed. The three are bunkered behind the crescent-moon reception desk that has never, in anyone's living memory, hosted an actual receptionist. Ritter keeps an eagle's eye on the front of the building as his brother loads shells into the feeding tube of a shotgun and Cindy idly sharpens the blade of her tactical tomahawk.

"What are you loading into that beast?" she asks Marcus.

"It's my own mix. Chupacabra teeth, dragon nail, and about ten bucks' worth of pure silver dimes. There's nothin' these sisters won't kill."

"Now, *that's* sexy."

Marcus grins.

"So," he begins, tentatively. "If we live through this . . . I mean . . . I'm gonna score, right?"

Cindy shakes her head. "Damn, boy, it's good to know you're bringing your A game for me."

"Jesus, Marcus," Ritter says under his breath, too embarrassed to look at either of them.

"C'mon! We're facing a pitched battle for our lives against overwhelming odds. It's the good guy underdogs versus the ultimate evil. All that shit. How does this not put me over the top, points-wise?"

"I'll take it under consideration," Cindy says, refusing to offer him even a subtle grin.

"That's all I'm requesting here."

"Are you done, you sad little man?" Ritter asks.

"You say 'sad,' I say I'm a man who has his priorities firmly—"

Ritter hisses at him to be quiet, his demeanor shifting subtly but noticeably into a far more urgent mode.

Marcus immediately falls silent and levels his shotgun, peering over the reception desk.

Cindy does the same, hefting her tomahawk in her dominant hand and unsheathing a large combat dagger with the other.

"What did you see?" Marcus whispers, the street appearing utterly serene to his eyes.

"Don't look, listen," Ritter instructs him.

It's a distinct whirring sound, faint at first, but growing louder and louder by the moment.

Through the lobby windows, all three of them watch as a giant battering ram, ripped free of its hulking metal host, twirls like a fourteen-foot baton down the street until it spears both the front and back windshields of a car parked on the curb in front of Sin du Jour, exploding both panes of safety glass and causing the car's alarm to screech and flash in protest.

For several moments, it's the only sound echoing in the lobby as the trio stares through the window in shock.

"The old man?" Marcus finally asks.

"Apparently, White Horse had more game than I ever gave him credit for," Cindy says.

Ritter activates the mystical security panel embedded in the reception desk with a wave of his hand.

Droopy Hound appears in the middle of the lobby, now clad in a firefighter's uniform.

"Things appear to be heating up, don't they, sir?" he asks, his nasal, dreary tone belying the play on words.

"Seal the building," Ritter orders him.

"I'm afraid I can't do that, sir."

"What do you mean, you can't?" Ritter demands. "You damn sure did before. I was ready to try and run through a brick wall because of you."

"Something is interfering with my ability to cast those protective fields, sir. Something more powerful than the charms over which I was given control."

"Well, shit," Cindy says

"What the hell *can* you do, then?" Marcus asks the demonic cartoon.

The scantest grin spreads through Droopy Hound's saggy jowls.

"I can watch, sir," he says before his animated form fills with static and fades from view.

"I'm gonna ace that fuckin' dog, I swear," Marcus promises.

"Later," Ritter says. "Right now, we hold the line."

Outside, the procession of troop carriers begins rolling by. The first two speed up and disappear down the street, while the third screeches to a halt directly before the front entrance.

Ritter watches the other two go. "They're headed around back!"

"That's not our gig," Cindy says. "We hold the lobby. You just told us. Everybody gonna have to do their part."

Ritter nods, knowing she's right even if the uncertainty of what's about to happen to the others twists his guts into balloon-animal shapes not found in nature.

Figures begin piling out of the troop carrier, rushing towards the entrance. It's too dark outside to make out anything except stray heads of blond hair, but none of them appear to be carrying weapons and all of them possess human, or at least bipedal, silhouettes.

"Party time," Marcus says, lining up the sights of his

shotgun, centering the entrance.

They begin breaking through the lobby doors and windows like something from an old zombie movie. As glass breaks and wood shrapnel rips free, Ritter, Cindy, and Marcus begin to spy identical red faces and irradiated gold hair like birds' nests perched atop human skulls. All of them are clad in the same dark suits and red ties.

"Okay, then," Cindy calmly assents. "We're being set upon by a horde of the cotdamned POTUS. Fine."

"They're meat puppets with gremlin drivers!" Ritter yells above the commotion. "Go for the sternum!"

The double doors break free of their hinges and topple to the lobby floor. Half a dozen presidential meat puppets pour through the entrance while another half-dozen begin climbing through the shattered windows.

Marcus takes aim at the one farthest out front and shoots him in the chest. The force of the shotgun's output literally knocks the meat puppet out of his shoes and splatters the walls with gelatinous, bloodless shrapnel. The body hits the floor, motionless, the front of its torso half-hollowed by the blast. A tiny, three-pronged green claw reaches out from inside that cavity, trembling and running with iridescent green blood.

As Marcus racks the shotgun and sets his sights on the next, Cindy lets loose a blood-curdling battle cry and leaps over the reception desk at the throng of meat puppets shambling from the windows on the other side of the room. She quickly spins like a discus thrower and impales the closest one through the center of its chest with her dagger's blade. The meat puppet doesn't fall; it simply stops moving, slumping forward on its feet like a powered-down automaton. At the same time, Cindy swings her tomahawk into the chest of another one.

Behind the reception desk, Ritter reaches inside his pocket and then holds his balled fist in front of his face. Opening his fingers, he reveals five small multicolored thumbtacks, like the kind you'd purchase at any ordinary office supply store. Ritter whispers several inaudible words to the tacks in a language that no longer exists. When he's finished, he very gently blows into his palm.

The thumbtacks immediately fly from his hand as if they were bullets leaving the barrel of a pistol. Each one finds its way into the center of a different meat puppet's chest, burrowing deeply there and finding the gremlins driving the POTUS clones.

"Fucking show-off," Marcus mutters, racking the slide and blasting one of the last targets still standing in the lobby.

"Go with what you know," Ritter says.

Marcus discharges another spent shell. "Hey! You know what I just realized, man?"

Ritter is already reaching for more tacks. "What's that?"

His brother sights his fourth and final meat puppet with a grin. "This is the closest I've ever come to voting!"

Ritter actually cracks a grin of his own, which is rare enough for him, but it's even more short-lived than his brother would've expected.

"What?" Marcus asks, his mirth quickly fading as he follows Ritter's dark gaze.

"That was just the first wave," Cindy calmly announces.

Sure enough, twice as many presidential meat puppets are swarming from the caravan outside and lumbering toward the broken windows and battered-down doors of the lobby, their identical faces seeming even redder and more bloated than usual.

Marcus racks his shotgun and checks the ammo bag attached to his belt, realizing he'll be depleted faster than they'll run out of racist rhetoric–spouting, bird's nest–haired enemy clones.

Ritter watches him, then looks back at the descending horde.

"It's time to fall back," he says.

# CHANGED

The thing under the large stained canvas tarp smells so foul, Moon actually considers asking Ryland for one of his cigarettes just so he can taste something else.

The two of them stand outside Sin du Jour's service entrance, looking like the least qualified sentries ever tasked with guarding a portal.

"Explain to me once more why I've agreed to this," Ryland says around the butt of his unfiltered Camel.

"Because . . . uh . . . all of the tires on your crap mobile home are busted and you can't drive away?"

"There is a certain rationale to that, admittedly."

"Listen . . . you've been a good teacher. I've been meaning to thank you."

"Please, spare me the threat of a bonding moment. I haven't the facilities to internalize such things. It's very much like when I ingest Mexican cuisine."

Moon can't help but grin. "All right, whatever. Thanks, though."

Ryland takes a long drag of his cigarette and blows enough smoke to populate a cock-rock music video from the 1980s.

"You've proven an adequate pupil," he says a moment later. "Far better than I was in your position."

"Wow. Thanks, man."

"It's hardly high praise, just so you know."

"Yeah, I get it. Still, thank you."

The lights of the armored carrier are blinding as it turns and barrels down the alley towards the service entrance.

"Is all that necessary?" Ryland complains, shielding his raw, red eyes with his forearm.

"Shit, dude, they're coming!"

The carrier accelerates to top speed and Ryland, still hiding his eyes, is spared the sight of the vehicle smashing into his booted RV. The old and decrepit Winnebago is practically ripped in half by the military transport, each section being knocked off its inert wheels and toppled to the cement. The carrier screeches to a halt upon impact. It appears totally unharmed after the collision, despite being parked amidst the smoking debris of what's no longer recognizable as a recreational vehicle.

Ryland slowly lowers his arm, hungover eyes blinking at the scene of the wreck.

"Fuck, dude, I'm sorry," Moon says.

"I suppose it was inevitable. Even overdue, dependent upon your perception of our ongoing circumstance."

A dozen humans clad in black flak jackets, helmets, and face masks deploy from the carrier with trained and uniform efficiency. They're all carrying assault rifles, and in the next moment, all of those assault rifles are pointing at Moon and Ryland.

"Stand aside from the door and lie down on the cement!" one of the faceless shock troops orders them both.

"And who are you to marshal me about?" Ryland demands as if they aren't all cradling fully automatic weapons. "This is precisely why I rejected military service, I'll have you know. You're bloody brimming with unearned grandeur, the lot of you."

As he talks, both he and Moon deftly grasp the changing medallions hung from chains around their necks; the one Ryland wears is the same one fashioned by his father and donned in his beloved Polaroid.

"Down on the ground or we'll light you up right now!" the armed operator repeats.

"Suck my ass, ya goon!" Moon fires back at him.

"Not entirely eloquent, but the sentiment is right," Ryland mutters.

A dozen fingers tighten around a dozen triggers, but before they can squeeze out a single round, four of the armed men are seized by a thousand micro-convulsions that wrack their bodies, causing them to lose their grips on their rifles. The others turn toward them, surprised and confused. Through their armor it's difficult to see the life being drained from the bodies of the four men, but the sight of their eyes sinking back into their skulls is unmistakable.

As they drop to the pavement, the large shape beneath the tarp in front of Ryland and Moon begins to stir. The mercenaries are so focused on their comrades, they don't notice until a jarring growl pulls their attention to the commotion just in time to watch the canvas flung back by the enraged grizzly that is now rising to full height.

The bear is enormous, still marred by a nasty head wound that should be and was fatal, and it appears to be incredibly pissed off.

"Fire!" the lead operator shouts, but by the time the first round has entered the bear's body, the monstrous creature is already on top of them.

"You'll have to forgive him!" Ryland shouts at the shock troops amiably. "He was killed by a hunter, so I imagine he's still quite cross at men with large rifles. You'll all understand, of course."

The reanimated creature given new life that was drained from those four shock troops shreds through the body armor and helmets of the rest of the men like giftwrapping, absorbing every bullet fired at its body. Each shot only seems to further feed its fury. By the time only one of the operators is left standing, the bear is bleeding from countless wounds and the lone gunman has run out of ammo.

The grizzly doesn't make it quick, and the mercenary isn't quiet about his feelings on the matter.

"That is *not* a fit sight for decent people," Ryland says, looking away.

"You never been to a horror movie?" Moon asks him.

"You aren't allowed to consume alcohol in most modern American theaters."

The screaming finally ceases. As the bear rears back and growls triumphantly at the night, an equally circular shape momentarily blots out the moon. When the shape descends, the rays of the exposed moon perfectly illuminate a solid metal sphere the size of a giant beach ball obliterating the bear's head. The sphere cracks the cement as it lands atop the pavement, splashing Ryland and Moon with bloody entrails upon impact.

"What the fuck?" Moon exclaims.

The sphere breaks apart into several dozen tiny pieces. Squinting, Moon and Ryland see the pieces are actually miniscule bipedal creatures wearing sleek, curved armor designed to fit together. Moon immediately recalls the kitchen staff's tales about the Japanese businessmen from the elemental banquet who were actually composed of dozens upon dozens of disguised . . .

"Gnomes," Moon says.

"I take it these miniature fellows are not on our side, then?" Ryland asks.

As if in answer to his question, Ryland yelps around his cigarette, his shoulders involuntarily jumping as he's struck in the chest by an unseen object. Blinking rapidly, he reaches a hand inside his shirt and feels around for a moment before retrieving a slender sprig of metal the size and shape of a toothpick. Ryland inspects it closely with a drunken, curious expression on his face, not noticing the blood beginning to seep through his breast pocket.

"I appear ... it appears I've been ... impaled ... by a very, very tiny sword. Funny, that."

"Dude, no" is all Moon manages before Ryland collapses in a heap of rumpled clothes and mussed hair.

Moon looks down at his motionless form. The cigarette is still perched perilously between Ryland's lips. It remains there, tendrils of smoke curling into the night air, the only spark still present in the man's body.

Even Ryland's death proved to be a pratfall.

Moon turns his tear-stung eyes to the gnomes, breath coming in shallow, angry bursts.

"You motherfuckers!"

The gnomes respond by rushing and leaping at each other, interlocking their armor and forming up into a single bipedal shape, like a slender clockwork knight. The warrior made of gnomish bodies advances on Moon, who backs up futilely until he realizes there's nowhere to go. A metal arm composed of armored gnomes rises threateningly above Moon's head.

"Fuckin' fine," he says in a ragged, desperate voice. "Do it. I did what I could. I tried. I'm ready. Fuckin' do it! See if I even care, you little butt plugs!"

Moon shuts his eyes tight, waiting.

He opens them when he hears the sound of a car crash directly in front of his face. What he glimpses is his gnomish would-be killers being flung in every direction after another large sphere has run through their interlocked form like a cannonball.

Moon has to duck and curl into a ball to avoid being hit by flying, screaming gnome shrapnel. He peers out of the corner of his eye, watching the new sphere bounce off the alley wall, hit the pavement, and roll to a halt. This metallic ball isn't made of sleek, clean, perfect curves like the steel one that re-killed their bear. This new sphere is rusted, battered, and misshapen. When it collapses into a hundred tiny bodies, Moon recognizes the shaggy beard tufts and banged-up armor.

"Hey, it's you guys!" he shouts jubilantly. "Dude, how'd you get here from Ireland? Do they let you fly commercial?"

Fortunately for Moon, the normally subterranean gnomes are too preoccupied to answer him. In the next moment, an all-out gnomish war has erupted in the alley of Sin du Jour, the faction of old-school elemental gnomes who refused to leave the earthen caverns they love battling the gnomes that have integrated into human society, forging themselves into perfect replica constructs of businessmen to enjoy aboveground luxuries.

Moon tucks himself into the archway of the service entrance and watches the fracas unfold, only one thought dominating his mind.

*I am not eating one of these things. Not again. I don't care which way it goes. Never again.*

# UNLOADING

A white-smock battalion has massed on the platform of the Sin du Jour loading dock. In truth, they look rather absurd, like a poorly themed gang from the movie *The Warriors*, but every single one of them is willing to fight and die to protect the others and their surrogate home. The entire kitchen staff, led by Dorsky and Nikki, has armed themselves for combat—Rollo with his medieval meat cleaver the size of a battleaxe, Tenryu wielding matched tsuba knives, Chevet two meat mallets, and James the same pitchfork he used to bale gourmet hay for their Taurus clientele.

Beside him, Darren has wrapped his fists the way Ritter taught him. His taped hands are choking the handle of a shovel.

"I really wish you'd take off," Dorsky says to Nikki, nervously shifting the grip of a gargantuan butcher's knife from one hand to the other. "At least go chill out with Boosha in her hole. It's probably the safest place in the building, not that that means much."

Nikki finishes pulling on a large reflective glove, three

times the size of a standard oven mitt.

She pats him on the chest with it. "Tag, you've come so far in such a short time. Don't revert back to a misogynistic pig now."

"It's not because you're a girl!" he insists. "A woman, I mean. It's not because of that. It's because I—"

He quickly stops himself because that part of him hasn't yet changed enough to allow such words to flow freely.

Nikki smiles sympathetically. "It's tough feeling things, huh?"

Dorsky drops his chin to his chest. "Yeah."

She reaches up with both mitt-covered hands and grips the sides of his face, tilting his head back to look into his eyes.

"Me, too," she says.

"Will you two get room?" Rollo fires at them.

"Leave them alone," James chides Dorsky's second-in-command.

"I understand, Rollo," Nikki says. "He was yours before he was mine."

The entire line laughs at that.

Even Rollo cracks a grin beneath his grizzly beard.

They hear the crash emanating from the front of the building through the exit to the delivery bay. It kills any lingering laughter immediately.

"All right, cowboy up, everybody!" Dorsky instructs them.

Nikki clears her throat sharply.

"Or cowgirl," Dorsky corrects himself. "Whatever. They're coming. Get ready."

As the chefs tighten their ranks, renewing their grips on their various armaments, they see the lights shining outside the entrance to the loading dock. A moment later, they hear one of the troop carriers turn into the bay, cutting a sharp right, its tires screeching across the pavement as it angles the side of the vehicle in front of the dock. The carrier's reinforced armored plating opens up, and every muscle on the platform tenses.

Rather than a squadron of heavily armed mercenaries or mystical monsters, however, one lone figure emerges from the vehicle.

Dorsky vocalizes their collective confusion. "What the hell is this?"

The woman is of middle age, draped in sheer black silk with a leather bodice visible underneath.

Several of the line cooks who were there recognize her from Enzo Consoné's disastrous inauguration. She was representing the witch covens, some kind of presiding elder among that group.

There is no coven with her now, however. She appears to be completely alone.

The witch takes in the sight of them clinging to each other and their makeshift weapons of war. She looks them over and she laughs, just a little, and just for a moment.

"Well, now," she says, resting her fists against her hips. "*You* are the rebels causing Allensworth so much bother? How quaint and thoroughly unbelievable."

"You're not welcome here," Nikki says. "We don't want any trouble, and no one here wants to hurt you. You can just go."

The witch stares up at her atop the loading dock with the bemused gaze of a parent being talked down to by an overenthusiastic child.

"I see," she says. "You don't want to hurt me . . . with what? Those sharp things in your hands?"

She raises her arms in front of her, wrists pressed together as if bound. The witch spreads her arms; every handle grasped in their hands flies loose from their fingers. Every blade sails from their grip, twirling across the space and either bouncing off the cement walls or embedding their edges in its surface. In one motion, the witch has disarmed the entire kitchen staff.

"Sad little creatures," she says. "Know your betters, and bow to them."

The witch drops her arm, and as she does, each one of their bodies is crushed to the deck of the loading dock.

It's as if gravity has increased by half. Several of the chefs are knocked unconscious by the fall, and all of them have the wind belted from their lungs.

The witch points a talon-nailed finger at Dorsky.

"Let's begin with you."

# SEND IN THE CLOWNS

"It's probably a shit time for sentimentality," Marcus says, panting, "but I missed running and gunning with you, man."

He punctuates the statement by leveling his shotgun behind them with one hand and unleashing a blind blast into the pursuing meat puppets.

Ritter only grunts a reply as they continue beating feet through the corridors of Sin du Jour with a legion of the worst President in United States history shambling after them.

"Y'all are precious," Cindy remarks, her breathing less taxed than either of them. "Truly. You need to work on your cardio, though."

"I do better when I'm not being chased, but that's just the way when you roll with this guy," Marcus assures her. "This one time, we were zip-lining away from these nasty-ass tree sprites and our line broke—"

"Save it!" Ritter orders him.

"I'll tell you later," Marcus whispers to Cindy.

She can't suppress a grin. "Can't wait."

The trio rounds the next corner and collectively spots two diminutive figures awaiting them at the center of the corridor. Jett, sans her usual war mask of perfect makeup and hair bound in a tight bun, is dressed down in her sharpest cage-fighter gear complete with the same fingerless mixed martial arts gloves she used to rain down punishment upon the succubus who infiltrated Sin du Jour and attempted to usurp her position. The only vestige of her typical work ensemble is the fleshy, growth-looking appendage affixed to her ear like a Bluetooth device that allows her to control her undead (or as Jett insists, "living-challenged") event workforce.

Pacific lingers behind her, scraggly blond hair tied back into an unusually formal ponytail and wearing his best busboy uniform. Despite the dressy garb, in typical Pacific fashion, he's casually puffing on an expertly rolled blunt.

"Jett!" Ritter shouts to her. "It's time! Turn 'em loose! Do it now!"

"This is gonna be so gnarly," Pacific comments through a cloud of smoke.

Sin du Jour's dutiful event planner nods with a steel-reinforced expression on her face and turns to the large metallic barn-style door affixed to the wall beside her. Someone has graffitied its patina-covered surface with

ALRIGHT SHAMBLERS, LET'S GET SHAMBLIN'. The door is secured with a thick chain and combination lock. Jett quickly disarms the lock and slips its U bend free of the links, yanking the length of chain through the door's handle and whipping it aside. Pacific purses his lips securely around the end of his blunt and uses both hands to aid Jett in sliding the heavy slab of metal aside.

Light pours into the otherwise darkened corridor. It's an eerie-enough addition to the setting even before the first zombie clown stalks out of the room behind the security door. He's a ghastly, macabre parody of the once popular Henley's fast food chain mascot, Redman Britches. Every Henley's in New York City has been shuttered for months since the corporation behind the franchise filed for bankruptcy amidst a massive and crippling class-action lawsuit verdict. Hundreds of people sued the chain after biting into their signature fried, breaded Chicken Nuggies and tasting battered bits of a human body instead.

The first zombie clown to shamble out of the room is followed by a dozen more undead versions of Redman Britches the Clown, some of average height and build, some tall and thin, some short and fat, and all of them in various states of decay corroding their once-vibrant painted faces. The first dozen are followed by a dozen more, until the corridor is packed with them.

Jett touches the organic device covering her right ear and whispers arcane words that are definitely not English. The zombie clown horde lurches forward in perfect step with one another, dragging their feet toward Ritter, Marcus, and Cindy, who run at them without fear. The trio sprints through the center of the horde and weaves deftly around their decrepit forms, the zombies ignoring their presence utterly. A moment later, the three of them join Jett and Pacific behind the advancing walkers.

"You okay, brahs?" Pacific asks with genuine concern.

Ritter hunches over and grips his knees, breathing slowly through his nostrils and exhaling from his mouth. He closes his eyes for a moment before opening them again to regard Pacific.

"Just another day at the office."

Marcus pats him on the back, motioning down the hall.

"It's about to be worth the jog," he says.

The presidential meat puppets actually halt as they find their way barred by dozens of zombie clowns choking the corridor.

"Talk about an epic smackdown," Pacific says with childlike excitement.

Marcus leaps high enough to see beyond the heads of the undead Redman Britches actors, yelling at the meat puppets, "Come and get us, ya fuckin' Nazis!"

The gremlin pilots inside the meat puppets no doubt take ultimate offense at that accusation, gremlins being the most blindly patriotic of all domestic supernatural creatures.

The President clones steel themselves and charge headlong at the zombie clown horde, gargling unintelligible cries issuing from their mouths.

"Eloquent as ever!" Marcus shouts through his cupped hands.

The meat puppets collide with the Redmans at the forefront of the horde, battering them with their bare, swollen fists. The Presidents strike down several clowns before the rest surge forward and close in on them, the undead clawing and biting the artificial flesh of the meat puppets, tearing into them like rabid dogs attacking a battalion of foam CPR dummies. It quickly becomes a dogpile of inhuman shells falling over each other like angry cannibalistic lobsters in a tank. The zombie clowns don't stop eviscerating the meat puppets until they've rooted out the gremlins driving them. Some are lucky enough to scurry away and skitter for their lives; others aren't lucky at all.

Soon, bloodless flesh-colored chunks decorated with ripped pieces of suit are splattering the walls and ceiling as if being spat from a wood chipper. The grotesque, violent pile-up becomes more rotting clown than puffy blowhard politician as the meat puppets are swallowed beneath the horde.

Marcus slaps his brother across the shoulder. "I *told* you it would be worth going back for these guys. As soon as Cindy recapped your whole Henley's heist for me, I fuckin' told you!"

Ritter continues watching the melee. "Uh-huh."

"The boy is impetuous," Cindy tells him, "but he has good ideas."

Pacific takes a final, drawn-out hit off his waning blunt and rubs the remnants of the paper between his fingertips to extinguish them.

"You don't see that kind of shit every day," he says. "Even workin' here."

"I'm just happy some of that untouchable white-privilege karma of yours rubbed off on the rest of us," Cindy says.

Pacific shrugs. "I just go with the flow, brah."

"Statistically, Zen management techniques have a noted effect on productivity and morale in corporate settings," Jett offers.

Cindy shakes her head. "Y'all make me feel like I'm multilingual sometimes."

Pacific giggles, but Jett only furrows her brow.

"I don't get it."

"That's my point," Cindy says.

# LOOK AT ME

Bronko and Lena watch from their rooftop station. They watch the battering ram whip down the street and lance the parked compact. They watch the troop carriers stream after it. They watch the horde of orange-faced meat puppets storm the front entrance. They rush across the blacktop to watch the troop carrier scream out of sight into the loading dock, and the other tear up the back alley toward the service entrance. They hear the metal thundercrash of the wreck, and from their vantage point, they glimpse Ryland's RV slammed against the alley wall in two mangled halves.

"Maybe we should get downstairs," Lena says desperately, her whole body aching to take action. "Reinforce the line in the loading dock, or back up Ryland and Moon. I mean, it's a lush and a slacker against who knows—"

"Ryland can handle his own self," Bronko assures her with the icy calm of thirty years leading large kitchens. "We're up here for a reason, same as they're down there for a reason. They gotta hold theirs; we gotta hold ours.

I know you sense a fight and the soldier in you says you should be in the thick of things, backin' up your buddies, and I feel ya on that, but our job is up here. Stuff it down and stay calm. We'll see action yet, I promise you."

Lena takes her executive chef's lead and follows his instructions as she always does, tamping down her adrenaline-fired need to move and trying to breathe slow and evenly.

"Yes, Chef."

"We'll see action yet," he repeats, more to himself than to her.

Bronko looks back across the rooftop. It's the same rooftop upon which half the Sin du Jour staff battled and defeated a demon assassin version of Santa Claus and his monstrous elves. It's the same rooftop upon which they held Hara's funeral. It's also vulnerable to any matter of nasty things Allensworth could summon that take to the air. And if the lines being held downstairs fail and the staff is pursued through the building, the roof is the only place they'll have to retreat.

Either way, something's coming and this rooftop must be secure, so it's where Bronko and Lena need to be.

He walks over to the roof's single access, opening the old but thick and sturdy metal door. The stairwell beyond is empty, quiet. The interior of the building beyond the stairwell, what Bronko can hear of it, is quiet too.

Whatever chaos is occurring at those ground-floor access points being guarded by the others has yet to sweep through the rest of Sin du Jour.

Lena watches him. "Are you feeling it too, Chef?"

Bronko snorts, offering her a wry grin. "I'm feelin' it all, Tarr. Every bit of it."

Lena smiles at him, taking genuine comfort and solace from his always easy, irrepressible manner, no matter the situation. The smile slowly fades as she watches an inexplicable spiral of bright red blossom in the center of Bronko's chest, the stain quickly spreading through the cotton capillaries of his white chef's smock.

He looks down at it curiously, detached from the sensation. When his brain finally receives the report from his body, Bronko awkwardly begins sucking in air and his eyes begin to glaze over.

Allensworth leans over Bronko's shoulder, speaking directly into his ear from beneath the hood of the cloak.

"This is what it feels like to be stabbed in the back, Byron."

"Chef!" Lena cries, rushing forward in panic and rage to maul Allensworth with her bare hands.

He uses his lethal leverage on Bronko to swing the former linebacker's massive frame into Lena, who collides with what feels like a brick wall. She's bounced down onto the rooftop, landing awkwardly on her hip and kidney, gasping for breath.

Allensworth disengages from Bronko's back, prompting the larger man to grimace and groan. Bronko slumps to his knees, then onto his side.

Lena sees that Allensworth's right hand has become a clawed reptilian thing, the talons slathered in Bronko's blood.

"Incidentally, Byron," he says, removing a scroll from inside his cloak and unfurling what looks like a contract prop from a community-theater staging of *Faust*. "I'm taking it upon myself to release you from our arrangement."

Allensworth draws one of those razor talons through the center of the contract, slicing it cleanly in half.

As he does, a stale, hot wind blows through the severed pieces of parchment, as if something has been released from its compressed state.

Allensworth lets the pieces flit to the black rooftop.

"What the fuck *are* you?" Lena asks, pushing away from the roof with her hands and standing slowly.

"Enhanced," he answers cryptically. "Thanks to you, Miss Tarr."

Allensworth draws back the hood of his cloak. More than half his face has been overtaken by the aspect of a demon, one eye yellowed and thinned in shape, tough, sickly green/brown hide replacing much of his usually perfectly coiffed hair. The right side of his mouth is wider, and the teeth curving over his lower lip are more like fangs.

"Don't worry, Miss Tarr; I've brought a gift for you, as well."

Allensworth's still-human hand delves beneath his cloak and produces a long shock of white hair, bits of bloody scalp still clinging to one end.

He tosses it at her feet.

"The old Navajo was full of surprises, I will attest. I had meant to batter down the walls of this decrepit tomb myself and exterminate you all level by level, saving Byron and yourself to the last, but he forced me to alter my plans. This worked out nicely, however. The rest of your Saturday-detention friends will be a lovely digestif. I'm only sorry you won't be around to witness it, to experience what that feels like. The knowledge it's going to happen is vastly different from watching it occur. Don't you find that to be true, Miss Tarr?"

Lena doesn't answer him. Instead, she draws a large knife; not a chef's knife but the kind she carried in Afghanistan, a knife designed as much for fighting and killing as utility.

Allensworth smiles a horrific, lopsided smile that brings that demonic visage through to the other side of his face.

"Excellent," he says. "Truly excellent."

She lets the rage and pain and malice fill her, checking nothing, denying nothing. Lena lets all of that hate saturate her every cell, flooding her brain and muscles with deliciously savage chemicals. When Lena charges him, her charge is feral, and so lost in it is she that the screams pouring from her own lips don't register in her ears. She swipes wildly at Allensworth with the knife, the half-demon puppet master backpedaling from the attack quickly.

Three feet from the roof's edge, he steps forward and takes a single, powerful swipe at her with his lethal talons. Lena ducks under his arm and immediately thrusts forward with her knife hand, a jubilant shock running through her as the blade finds purchase, sinking deeply into flesh.

That jubilance just as quickly fades when Lena realizes she's speared the meat of that demon hand, Allensworth managing to intercept the thrust with the center of its palm; worse, she realizes she can't jerk the blade free of the unnatural appendage, no matter how hard she pulls or cries out in frustration.

He draws his demon hand away and strikes the side of her face, the blade of Lena's knife opening the flesh of her cheek. She doesn't see the rooftop rushing up at her, but she feels its impact. In the next moment, he's on top of her, the weight of his body crushing and immovable. Lena can't move her legs, let alone put up her guard. Allensworth rips her knife free of his changed flesh and casts it away, wrapping that demon claw around her throat, the strength of its grip shocking in its power, immediately cutting off her air supply.

"You realize, of course, the fallacy in your central conceit. You still believe this story is about you, all of you, a pile of lowly cooks, secondhand mercenaries, and cut-rate magicians. This is the beginning of *my* story, Miss Tarr. It is the story of my eventual and inevitable ascension. You and the others, you're a small part of the prologue to that story. It's now time for the prologue to end."

Allensworth cinches his scaly fingers around her neck, watching the flesh of her face darken to a shade of red bordering on purple.

"And now it ends," he says.

The world goes silent for Lena. She can't feel anything except the hemorrhaging gash in her cheek, raised and aching and running hot with blood. The sight of Allensworth's monstrous, utterly euphoric expression as large and looming as the sun directly above her begins to distort in Lena's vision.

Although she technically does see the pressed steel head of the shovel collide with Allensworth's skull, Lena's conscious mind doesn't really register it. The same is true for Allensworth's demonic hand leaving her throat and the weight of his body vanishing from atop hers. She experiences these things, but reality is still a stunted haze, and it's only after her lungs reinflate and she's dry-heaved for several moments that the sound of the world around her returns and her brain begins to catch up.

The first thing she's truly aware of is Bronko lying on his back several yards away, not moving. She is beginning to crawl toward him when a disturbing gargling noise and a familiar voice growling hateful words draw her attention in the opposite direction.

Darren is kneeling over Allensworth's prone form, one of his knees pinning the wrist of Allensworth's demon hand to the rooftop. Both of Darren's hands are wrapped around the man's mutated neck. Allensworth seems utterly helpless beneath Darren's ministrations, a fact Lena can't reconcile, considering the otherworldly power she felt in Allensworth's grip just a moment ago.

"Look at me!" Darren commands him. "Remember what you did to me! Think about what you did and look at me! *I'm* doing this to you. Do you understand that? Do you hear me? I want that to be the last thing on your mind. I want you to remember what you did to me while you watch me fucking kill you. I want that to be the *very last thing* you think about before you die, you son of a bitch!"

Lena weakly raises her arm, extending her hand toward Darren and opening her mouth to voice some kind of protest. The words never come. Some part of her brain knows what's happening in front of her needs to happen, but the image of Darren in that state, the fury and violence so unlike him, is enough to prompt another part of her to want to stop it from going any further.

The sound of Allensworth's bones crunching as Darren's inhumanly strong grip tightens and crushes his neck is loud enough to be heard clear across the rooftop, and it lasts until there isn't a shard of bone left that's large enough to shatter.

Darren doesn't loosen his grip, even after both of Allensworth's eyes are threatening to pop from their sockets and his body has gone completely slack. Darren's breathing is so heavy and so shallow that spittle is flying from his mouth, and his every muscle is visibly trembling.

"Darren, he's dead," Lena whispers. "He's dead. It's over. Stop. Please."

His fists unclench. Darren finally exhales one long, labored breath, leaning back and letting his face turn to the night sky, the peace and serenity that cover them there contrasting the violent scene.

"Darren . . . how did you . . . how did you do that?" she asks him, eyes transfixed by Allensworth's neck, which looks like a discolored, deflated balloon.

"I still have the strength," he whispers to the sky. "I still have whatever he gave me so I could kill for him. That hasn't gone away. I don't know why. Maybe it'll go away too after a while. Maybe it's just part of me now."

Lena nods, accepting that because her brain is too tired and too preoccupied to question it further. She turns away and crawls across the rooftop to where Bronko is sucking wind, staring at the stars much like Darren. Most of his smock is now dyed in his blood. She hovers over him, unsure where to even begin. Applying pressure to his chest wound will just pump blood from it faster and heavier.

"You're gonna be all right, Chef."

His voice is broken and ragged, but it still belongs to Bronko Luck. "Seein' this here smock is meant to be white and not red, I'm thinkin' I'm fucked, Tarr."

"Don't say that!"

"Not sayin' it won't undo it."

Frantic tears prick at the corner of her eyes. "Then you'll come back, right? You came back before. You'll—"

Bronko shakes his head. "Allensworth knew what he was doing when he eighty-sixed that contract. It's a one-way ticket this time."

"No—"

"I need you to listen to me now, girl. Okay? You remember . . . you remember Tunney? That old dishwasher I told you hipped me to you and Vargas needin' work? When I first called you?"

Lena nods.

"That was a big ol' lie. I knew . . . I knew about you. I had looked into it, researched you, who you were, where you'd been. I . . . I picked you."

Lena doesn't understand. "For what?"

"To replace me. You were who I chose. I made it so you'd have no choice but to work here. I'm sorry for that. I needed . . . I needed someone like me I can trust when the time came. You . . . had the stuff. I know I'm pickin' a helluva time to tell you, seeing as how you ain't rightly in a position to be mad at me—"

"Of course not, Chef," Lena assures him, tears streaming down her cheek, mixing with her blood.

"All you wanted since you been here was out, but now I need you to choose to stay. They're gonna . . . they're all gonna need you . . ."

She's still waiting for him to finish after her unconscious mind has registered that Bronko is dead. Eventually, she has no choice but to fully accept it, and then Lena is sobbing over her fallen mentor in the ugly, unbidden way only that kind of loss can evoke. She clutches his bloody smock and cries into his neck. Some time later, Darren's arms find her, his soft touch bearing none of the brutal strength with which he murdered Allensworth, and Lena allows herself to be held in those arms.

"There's nothing we can't come through the other side of," he says, his voice shaking as he takes in the sight of Bronko lying there before them. "I know that now. You will too. I promise."

Lena nods into his chest, but no words can stop her tears from flowing, not right now.

# SEAMS

Dorsky's body is pulled by unseen hands from the dock floor and hoisted into the air, where he remains, suspended.

"I'm afraid I'm a woman of very few words, young man. However, if anyone should ask you about this later, perhaps you could tell them I offered you a pithy heart-related pun first."

The material of Dorsky's smock rips apart over his torso. As he looks on, helpless, a bloody incision line begins trailing down the center of his chest. The witch's will splays his flesh as if she's performing some unnecessary surgery. He tries to stifle it, but a guttural and agonized howl escapes his throat. The slashed folds of his chest continue to pull away from each other.

A sudden mechanical hissing draws the witch's attention from Dorsky, whose torment is momentarily alleviated. She looks down at the deck just in time to watch Nikki blast her with the same mad-scientist liquid-nitrogen cannon she used to freeze the fire elementals' food. The witch is quickly engulfed in freezing smoke, her surprised shrieking all that remains of her for a moment before that, too, ceases.

Nikki empties the canister on her. When the cloud of smoke clears, the woman's bent and hunched-over form is one misshapen block of ice. What's visible of her face is twisted into an expression of agony.

Nikki drops the cannon to the deck, her own body slumping in relief. She begins crawling across the loading dock towards Dorsky, who is breathing shallowly on his back several yards away.

She's halfway to him when Nikki hears a brief, frantic rumbling. In the next moment, she's showered in icy fragments as the frozen matter encasing the witch explodes.

"That . . . was unpleasant," the older woman informs Nikki, sounding thoroughly unruffled.

Nikki feels her insides sinking in defeat.

"No . . ."

"Oh, my dear, you're the hopeful type, aren't you? Your kind always falls the farthest in these moments."

She raises that stiletto blade of a fingernail in Nikki's direction. In the next moment, the witch begins levitating into the air, spreading her arms wide. Nikki waits for what's coming, shying away from the sight of the malevolent woman, but Nikki remains lying unrestrained upon the deck.

Looking back at the witch, she realizes the woman

isn't levitating herself. The witch is being levitated by another, apparently more powerful force. The woman is suspended there, an expression on her face of shock and rage threatening to collapse into terror.

Behind the witch, Nikki watches a row of young women move inside the loading dock almost in formation. There are two dozen of them or more, most of them appearing to be younger than twenty-one. They're all dressed nondescriptly, in simple Old Navy sweaters and flannel shirts over tank tops with jeans or sweatpants. A more mature woman with hair curling past her waist Nikki doesn't recognize as Cassandra moves with them in the center of the row.

All of their eyes are focused on the coven elder suspended seven feet above the bay floor now. The witch is visibly trembling, her every muscle seeming to twitch uncontrollably.

"I finally see your point about solitaires, Melinda," Cassandra says to the other witch. "It appears it *is* better to have friends. And while we aren't a coven, we do all share one unifying thing. We all owe you and your kind *so much.*"

The witch, Melinda, can't even summon the voice to scream, such is her current agony.

Somehow, Nikki knows what's about to happen, and she looks away, shutting her eyes tight so there's no chance she'll be forced to retain the memory of what comes next.

When the witch is pulled apart at the joints, her arms and legs and head separating from the rest of her body, she finally finds her voice again.

Nikki feels hot teardrops spatter her neck and she knows they're the witch's blood, but she still doesn't look. She waits out the screaming and the even more horrific sounds she never knew human flesh was capable of making. She waits through several more seconds of silence just to be sure, and then opens her eyes.

Most of what's left of Melinda is sloshed across the loading bay floor in front of the dock. Somehow, it helps that it no longer looks like a body, but it doesn't help that much.

Suddenly, Nikki's brain screams, *Tag!*

She turns away from the gory scene and finishes her crawl to where Dorsky is sprawled atop the dock. He's staring wide-eyed at the fluorescent lights bolted to the ceiling, his entire torso awash in blood. His staccato breathing has become calm and sparse.

Nikki's hands hover over him without touching his body. She has no idea where to even begin. Her eyes are wide as well, but where Dorsky's are vacant, hers are filled with horror and shock.

"I tried," he's whispering with barely any voice left. "I really tried."

Nikki nods sympathetically, tears spilling over her lower eyelids. "I know you did, hon. I'm so proud of you."

His head begins to turn toward her, but before their eyes meet, it stops.

Nikki watches the life leave his body, as clearly as if she were watching him walk through a doorway. She reaches up with a trembling hand and touches his cheek with just the tips of her fingers, feeling the remnants of warmth there, and it's that warmth more than anything else in this moment that causes her to start sobbing.

Some time later, she's aware of a large body kneeling beside her. It's Rollo, his bushy beard wet with tears, though he weeps silently. They never lock eyes, but the embrace they share, clinging fiercely to each other, is a more meaningful exchange than any other they could have.

Nikki closes her flooded eyes against the bear of a man's chest, wanting to look down at Dorsky yet not wanting to see him like that again. She settles for the picture of him in her mind, smiling and cocky and trying to hide the fact he's not an asshole. She's at once sorry she saw through that exterior for the pain it's causing her now, yet grateful she did.

She hears his final words repeating in her head, and Nikki can't help thinking how all anyone can do is try, and how so often, despite that soulful effort, it's simply not enough.

# SITTING UP WITH THE DEAD

Little Dove knows he's gone.

It was supposed to be her and White Horse stationed together in the courtyard, the broken square of century-old cobbles and concrete open to the air between the four large rectangles of dusty red brick and gray mortar that compose Sin du Jour's headquarters. But her grandfather decided to play Gandalf battling the Balrog, leaving her alone in this darkened well of stale air and the remnants of a thousand company barbeques, and now she's certain he, after almost eighty years of wandering, just found his destiny. Little Dove feels his spirit travel beyond the intangible membrane separating this world from the next plane, then the next, and the next, leaving pieces of himself behind like echoes passing through many canyons.

When the first ghost comes to visit her, Little Dove is crying quietly in the dark.

The statuesque woman inexplicably standing in the courtyard reminds Little Dove of Jett, but lacking the open, earnest, and helpful demeanor of Bronko's most stalwart lieutenant. She wears eyeglasses with oversized ebony frames that match her smartly pressed pinstriped skirt suit and leather heels. Her hands are clasped formally in front of her, and she regards Little Dove with a practiced, brilliant, unshakeable, yet mirthless smile.

"Good evening," the woman says. "I don't believe we've had the pleasure. My name is Luciana Monrovio."

Little Dove quickly wipes her eyes with the backs of her palms, sucking in acrid-tasting snot.

"I know you," she says. "You're a . . . what-do-you-call-it . . . succubus. You tried to take us over."

"I formally served as liaison between Chef Luck and Mr. Allensworth, yes. Unfortunately, Chef Luck and I failed to achieve the appropriate synergy and our professional relationship was remaindered."

"I hear Jett beat the shit out of you."

The slightest tremor upsets Luciana's brochure-cover smile, but it is quickly forced under control.

"You're not . . . alive, are you?" Little Dove asks as if she's fully aware of the answer.

Luciana nods. "I have shuffled loose this mortal coil, yes."

"And you're not . . . I mean, you're here, but you're not *here*. You're a spirit."

"I am a noncorporeal entity, yes."

"Why are you still here?"

"I remain in Mr. Allensworth's service in my current and admittedly limited state."

"What do you want?"

"I want to murder your coworkers to the last sad, pathetic reject among their ranks. Immediately following that, I want to tear this eyesore down around their twisted, mutilated corpses."

She says all of these things without a hint of irony or malice, as if she's a mail carrier who has knocked at Little Dove's door and is informing her of a delivery.

And Luciana's smile doesn't falter.

Little Dove's tear-glazed eyes turn hard. Her right hand reaches for the deerskin pouch hanging around her neck, an early bequest from White Horse. He told her it was filled with pebbles from a sacred stream and eagle feathers, but when Little Dove opened it later that night, she found only a red-and-yellow Hot Wheels racing car that looked as though it'd been chewed up by a dog. She thought it was a joke, then remembered White Horse's lessons about the words and the artifacts mattering little, if at all; they were only props to activate the true power from within.

"And you started with my Pop," she says to Luciana.

"No, Mr. White Horse took it upon himself to force the issue and met his fate early, albeit awfully, I assure you."

Little Dove clenches her teeth so hard, her jaw trembles. She steps forward, still gripping the pouch hung around her neck.

"I'm going to send you somewhere just as fucking awful," she promises the spirit. "I know how."

"Oh, I'm sure you do, but if you would kindly wait a moment before initiating that process, it would be to your advantage. I will explain why."

"You are so goddamn annoying. I get why Jett broke your face."

"You stated previously you know me," Luciana says, unperturbed. "I am familiar with you, as well. Your juvenile record is quite extensive and includes several brief yet revealing reports from the counselors and social workers that interviewed you in your formative years. They paint a portrait of an angry young woman who, more than anyone, wishes to change who she is and above all, her current circumstance."

"I'm not a kid anymore."

"No, you've undergone a thoroughly 1980s coming-of-age film mystical transformation, haven't you? Under your late grandfather's tutelage, you've become quite the . . . Is *medicine woman* an offensive term? I would think it's a progressive concept among your people."

"I'm what my grandfather was," Little Dove says with conviction. "Hatałii, and I'm not the first woman to be that."

Little Dove becomes aware of another presence in the courtyard, and it causes her to shiver as if she's walked into an arctic frost.

"You're not alone, are you?" she asks Luciana.

Luciana's masking smile becomes more of a genuinely pleased grin. "Of course not. Mr. Allensworth has called in several favors and debts from beyond the veil, as it were. He's formed quite the elite spectral battalion, including several *entirely* infamous serial killers and at least one notorious dictator. I won't resort to name-dropping, but needless to say it's an A-list lineup."

"Then why are we talking?"

Luciana sighs. "The answer to that question is, ultimately, the reason for my visit. You see, as capable as our noncorporeal forces are, they . . . it seems . . . unanimously refuse to violate these premises, at least temporarily."

"Why?"

"You," Luciana says, trying and failing to hide her reluctance in making that admission.

Little Dove can't even attempt to process that.

"Me?"

Luciana hesitates for the scantest moment and then nods. "It appears there is a vast nexus of extradimensional power in this building, and the source of that power . . . apparently . . . is you. Not to belabor the matter or flatter your ego, but there isn't a malicious spirit on this plane of existence who is willing to cross you. We've searched."

"I don't believe that."

"Neither do I," Luciana admits, the irritation behind her words creeping through and bleeding into her expression.

She smiles anew, shrugging her padded shoulders. "But then, some people are simply born with ability they never earned. It is an unquantifiable fact of life."

"Are you afraid of me?" Little Dove asks, almost amused despite everything.

Luciana pauses, her delicate brow (or at least the astral projection of it) wrinkling.

"I find myself more curious than anything. However, I can *see* it in you, like a wellspring. It is much like looking upon a toddler carrying a bazooka. Although you've no doubt learned just enough about your natural gifts to be dangerous to . . . my particular subgroup."

"Then why don't you fuck off?" Little Dove spits at her, the brief amusement gone and unbridled vitriol replacing it.

Luciana sighs again. "I have a proposition to outline, and I would advise you to seriously consider it."

"No."

"Then simply begin by listening. You have strong feelings for your grandfather. I respect that. However, he is gone, or at least he's left behind his Earthly concerns. The truth is you never wanted to be here. You never wanted to be anywhere you've found yourself. You've been tethered to death and decay since birth. Your people, their reservation, your family. Here, you've found only more of the same, and there's more to come still. I understand your obligation to your grandfather, but what is your obligation to these people, especially now that he's gone?"

"They're my friends."

Luciana's grin turns lupine, almost predatory. "Are they, my dear? Why, because Miss Glowin taught you how to bake a cake? Because the women of this company enabled your underage drinking for their amusement? Because they patted your head when you told them your problems and offered you big-sisterly advice? Tell me, have any of them ever invited you into their homes or their confidence? Have any of them offered you any more than the courtesy that was convenient for them at the time? I regret to inform you that you are *not* their friend, young lady; you are their pet Indian girl. It's a tale as old as this sham of a country, I'm afraid."

Little Dove's breath is hot and elevated as she says, "I'm *not* an Indian; I'm Navajo."

"To them you're a novelty," Luciana insists. "Look at you now. They've left you alone, here, in the dark to face what comes without their aid or friendship. They've already forgotten about you."

"That's not true!"

"Then call to them," Luciana urges her. "Call to them for help and see if any of them come. Go ahead."

Little Dove says nothing. Her mind is suddenly racing through thoughts as ugly as Luciana's implications.

"We all knew what this was," she says quietly a moment later. "We all knew our jobs. We all knew . . ."

"You're making excuses for people who don't deserve your loyalty," Luciana says forcefully. "The tragedy is you're capable of so much more. You have power, young lady. It's rare and potent and *highly* valuable. It could attain for you literally *anything* you wish. You want to travel the world? You want wealth? You want respect? You want to meet famous people and have them *want* to know you and please you? I know you've thought about all these things. I know you hate dreaming about them, because it pains you too much to even visualize what you know you'll never have."

"Shut up!" Little Dove screams at her, new tears streaming down her cheeks.

"*I am trying to help you,*" Luciana insists. "I am offering you *everything*. Everything you've ever wanted. I work for the people who can make all of your repressed dreams a reality. I can give you everything you've ever wanted. You can have the life you truly deserve, far away from here where you'll never have to think about this pitiful company, its employees, or the troubles of your people and your family again."

"What do you want from me?" Little Dove says miserably, feeling the strength leaving her knees, wanting to crumple there on the cobblestones.

"I only want you to leave. That's all. Simply leave this place. Walk out of this building right now. You will not be harmed in any way. And in return, my employer will grant any wish you have, fulfill every desire you've ever harbored. It is more than a fair exchange."

Little Dove swallows hard, staring at the ground, unable even to meet the spirit's eyes for the shame of even asking, "And then what?"

Luciana shakes her head. "It doesn't matter. What happens after you leave this building will no longer be of any consequence to you. You'll never have to think about it again. I promise."

The other presence Little Dove felt before, a legion of spirits lingering at the periphery of her perception, begins to close in around her. She feels them all in that moment, hungry, raging, lost, and vicious. They sense her spirit weakening in that moment like sharks tasting blood in the water. They're suddenly so close, it's almost like feeling hot breath on her neck. Little Dove sees faces and shapes forming in the shadows draping her shoulders, ugly, mangled visages and monstrous aspects emerging from the dark around her and nipping toothless at her flesh, raising a hundred thousand microscopic bumps.

"Walk away, dear," Luciana says gently. "It's time to let all of this go and start living for yourself. You can do it."

Little Dove begins shaking her head, closing her eyes to stem the tears, but she feels something cracking in her head. She hears a voice, her voice, and it's the angriest part of herself demanding retribution for all the pain and loss and degradation Little Dove has endured since she was a small child. The voice is loud and powerful and salient enough to be convincing. So much of what Luciana says is the truth; she can't deny that. She's only ever wanted out. It's only been in the past few months, finally learning from her grandfather rather than nursing and protecting him from himself, that Little Dove has found release.

But what about the other nineteen years? What does she get for that? What is she owed for all of that time?

That angry voice answers her: *Everything*, it says. *Everything this spirit offers. We deserve that.*

All of a sudden, entertaining the thought of walking away doesn't even feel like betrayal to Little Dove. It feels natural, even inevitable. The more she envisions actually doing it, the more righteous she feels, and the more those malicious entities around her press in and whisper their assent.

*Fuck Sin du Jour*, she thinks.

She opens her mouth to speak, but a sharp pain jabbing up her arm cuts off the words. Little Dove realizes she's been gripping her deerskin pouch this whole time, and the edges of the little toy car inside have bitten into her palm. The pain and its source make her think of her grandfather's face, hard like stone and lined with the crags of what always seemed like eons, framed by those shocks of pure white hair that lost their color as a result of the things he was able to see that most mortals cannot.

Thinking about him does more than break through the turmoil within her; it seems to summon his voice, reaching through the spectral walls of the four worlds and funneling his words into her spirit. There he speaks the wisdom she needs in that moment, a final lesson from a true Hatałii and the man who raised her and taught her to be what she is now.

"No, fuck *this* bitch," White Horse says to her.

And he's right, of course. The hot moment of selfish release felt good, but as all indulgences are, it is utterly fleeting. It burns away, her angry fourteen-year-old self fading with it, and what's left is the Hatałii she's become and her conscience. Perhaps the girl would've fled, would've accepted Luciana's cheap bribery, but the woman will not be seduced. She sees the truth.

This is her home, and these are her people.

Little Dove cries out in the dark, letting loose a feral scream, and much more than that. Something gargantuan feels as though it is uncapped within her, like a rocky scab atop the mouth of a great geyser breaking apart. What pours forth from the "wellspring" Luciana spoke of is power Little Dove has yet to discover, a reservoir of it with no bottom. It is the power to command all that exists between worlds, the spirits clinging to a plane their flesh has abandoned.

The tidal wave sends the malevolent things surrounding her scattering in every direction, abandoning the battle for Sin du Jour in primordial fear.

Luciana adds an agonized shriek to Little Dove's cry as the succubus's spirit is dispersed in a sickly kaleidoscope of terrible light.

Little Dove drops to her knees, scraping them against the rough stones of the courtyard without feeling it, sobbing into her hands.

# LATE PREMIERE

The swaying access door is kicked out of the way, and Marcus and his shotgun storm the rooftop with military attitude, quickly clearing the space through the sights of his weapon. Ritter and Cindy follow, Ritter the first one to fully take in the sight of Lena and Darren kneeling over Bronko's blood-soaked body. Cindy and Marcus fall in behind him, the latter lowering his shotgun as the line cooks look up at them in anguish.

"What happened?" Ritter asks. "Who—"

Lena points behind them, at Allensworth's body with its nearly neckless head lolled unnaturally to the side.

"Is that Allensworth?" Cindy asks.

"Half of him, looks like," Marcus comments. "He must have gotten a transfusion of demon blood, or an organ or something. There was a brisk trade for that kind of shit in Thailand years back before they shut it down. This one time when we were in Bangkok—"

Ritter shakes his head severely at Marcus, the reprimand in his eyes deep and fierce.

Marcus quickly shuts up, nodding his contrition to his brother.

Lena and Darren stand as Ritter approaches them, staring down at Bronko's serene final expression. He crouches down slowly and rests a hand over the executive chef's forehead.

"He gave me a second chance," Ritter says. "I didn't even know it at the time, but . . ."

He just shakes his head.

"What's happening downstairs?" Lena asks, her voice hollow but her mind working at full speed.

"Looks like it's over," Ritter says, standing. "Everybody came through for us. Ryland's down. Moon's okay."

Ritter looks to Darren. "What about your line?"

"Everyone except Dorsky," he says, the absence of emotion in his voice somehow more powerful than if he'd delivered the news sobbing.

Lena blinks rapidly but finds there's little left for Dorsky inside of her at that moment. She knows it'll come later, in droves.

"Does anybody else hear that?" Marcus asks, providing her with a welcome distraction from her thoughts.

Lena looks away from the soul-gnawing scene at their feet, staring across the old and battered rooftops of Long Island City. The sleek, lighted bodies of newly built condos loom high among them like something ancient that had long lain in wait beneath the surface of the streets and finally burst through.

They all fall silent, listening to the night.

It may have been faint a moment ago, but now it's rising, the oppressive sound of heavy boots pounding the pavement far below in unison, a chorus that has scored millions of nightmares about armies coming for you and your loved ones in the dead of the evening. It's the sound of hundreds marching through the streets, and in the next moment they all feel the building beneath them quake, just a little, but the vibrations are strong enough to unsteady their feet and rattle their teeth.

Ritter is the first to break for the edge of the roof, Lena quick to follow behind him. The rest beat feet across the blacktop, joining them along the brick-lined ledge. They peer down together at the street in front of Sin du Jour's demolished main entrance. What they see flash-freezes their blood in an instant, stealing every last sliver of hope from their collective eyes.

Lena and Ritter find each other's gaze and they lock on tight, all the desperation and fear and pain and loss of the moment passing between them without a word.

"So, this is what it feels like," Marcus says quietly.

"What?" Cindy asks him.

He swallows what feels like a steel ball bearing before answering.

"Being well and truly fucked."

They fill the formerly deserted street, arranged in skirmish lines three rows deep that seem to totally surround the front and back alley of the building. Their sickly green-scaled faces shine hungrily and horrifically in the flame light of torchbearers flanking each column. They are all warriors of the Vig'nerash, the younger upstart demon clan Lena helped serve during her first event with Sin du Jour. Unlike the Oexial demons she fought at the disastrous movie premiere after-party that almost saw half of the kitchen staff burned at the stake, the Vig'nerash aren't clad in jagged pieces of brutal medieval-looking armor like something from Peter Jackson's *Lord of the Rings* trilogy. These are next-generation demons, integrated demons of the modern world. Every warrior is clad in dozens of stylish modular composite plates lain protectively over skintight bodysuits. Their weapons, pole axes and curved swords, look more like gargantuan Apple accessories than deadly blades. They possess the angular modern design aesthetic of a tech billionaire's foyer.

None of it is enough to distract from their bloated, diamond-scaled, horrifically snaggletoothed faces, however, or the lustful, hungry-for-blood look in their reptilian eyes.

Marcus looks down at the inhumanly compressed

neck of Allensworth's distorted corpse.

"I guess we're past negotiating, huh?" he observes.

"Sorry," Darren says, but it's a hollow sound without conviction.

"What's the play?" Cindy puts forth, trying to fill her voice with brass and authority that can't hope to weigh down the fear and futility she feels.

"We have to get back downstairs," Ritter insists. "We have to reinforce the others. They'll be overrun before they know what hit them."

Marcus looks at his brother incredulously. "And we won't?"

"What else can we do?" Ritter shoots back at him.

"You can't fuckin' *magic* us out of here or something, Mr. Wizard?"

Ritter's usually dour expression darkens several shades. "If you're ever going to grow up, this looks to be your last chance to do it."

"Fuck you!" Marcus thunders.

"Fuck you harder," Ritter says calmly.

Cindy turns from the ledge to face them both, exploding. "Will you cool it with this sibling Dr. Phil shit? Damn!"

A horn sounds in the distance, filling the streets below with a deep, primordial thrumming like something ancient calling to them through a tunnel made of bone.

"Shit!" Marcus swears, like the rest of them assuming it's the demons being called to charge. "Let's go!"

He turns to dash for the roof access door, but Ritter reaches out and grabs a handful of his shirt collar, stopping him.

When Marcus turns to curse at him, his brother points back down at the street, and what Marcus sees when he looks gives him the same pause.

The street is still congested with over-stylized reptilian warriors. The demons haven't budged. The winding of the horn hasn't called them to battle. Rather than charge, storming the building with teeth gnashing and artisan axes chopping, the attention of the demon horde seems to have been drawn *away* from Sin du Jour by the horn's bellow.

A different chorus begins to sing to them from the corners of the block. This symphony, however, isn't played by jackboots stomping in unison with genocidal intent. This is the music of bone dancing lightly on marble, the clacking of majestic hooves. They begin to hear stray whinnies and the smoky flare from equine nostrils wrinkling the air. Those noises are joined by the unmistakable sound of horses, a lot of them, clip-clopping over the city streets.

Lena and the others have to fight to rip their collective gaze away from the snake-toothed, designer armor–clad visage of destruction below.

"What the fuck is this?" Cindy says breathlessly, turning to Ritter. "Did you do that?"

He stares back at her, utterly speechless, and shrugs.

Dozens of white stallions, pure alabaster coats and flawless silver battle armor flashing bright and brilliant in the moonlight, have filled the intersections at either end of the street, bottle-capping the demon horde at both ends. The warriors astride each horse appear to be human, only way, way hotter, all of them, to a rider. Each head of perfectly coiffed hair gleams as brilliantly as the magnificent mounts beneath them. They wear the same sleek, angular silver armor protecting their steeds.

A light fills Lena's eyes, one she would've thought just a moment before could no longer be sparked within her.

"Holy shit," Marcus marvels. "The cavalry."

Ritter nods dumbly. "Literally."

"More like the goddamn red carpet at the Oscars," Cindy says, even more aghast.

Even at a distance, the famous faces of the mounted warriors are undeniable. Practically the entire starring cast of every big-budget superhero/heroine movie of the past decade composes the front line of the two battalions lined up across each intersection. Hollywood studio sets must look like ghost towns at this moment, or at least only scenes involving the main characters' best friends are being filmed.

Even the horses look prettier than regular horses.

Foot soldiers wait in the periphery, wearing lighter, more ceremonial armor and carrying halberds. Lena recognizes the garb from the goblin royal wedding catered by Sin du Jour. She also recognizes several of the foot soldiers from her favorite YouTube channels and realizes they all appear to be YouTube stars. She finds herself wondering if YouTube is the new boot camp for burgeoning goblin nobles, and immediately realizes what and on how many levels a bananas thought that is to have right now.

"What is this? Lena asks, half-convinced she's hallucinating the miraculous saving grace they all appear to be witnessing.

"It's the Royal Goblin Army," Ritter says without a trace of irony.

Lena shakes her head, more bewildered than she's ever been in her life. "That's seriously a thing?"

"For real?" Cindy echoes.

"I guess the goblins chose a side," Marcus says.

The demons begin closing ranks, re-forming *away* from the front of Sin du Jour's building and massing to face the army encroaching on both ends of the street.

"Hold the damn phone!" Cindy shouts with an entirely different energy than the shock and awe they're all experiencing.

A slight rider gallops up and down the goblin battalion line formed in the intersection closest to the building, raising high a short sword with a hilt forged in the shape of an iconic character millions know as the Love Symbol. He almost looks like a child on such a large mount, especially seen from the rooftop. Unlike the rest of the goblin soldiers, his armor is painted a royal purple, and its lines and edges have been forged with an eye toward dramatic flair. A high collar of steel curved at the top like the folds of a cape rises from the pauldrons bouncing on his virtually nonexistent shoulders and surrounds his head, yet somehow the man's downright majestic afro draws the eye far more.

Cindy grips Ritter's shoulder, digging her nails into him painfully without realizing. "Is that . . . that *can't* be!"

"It is," Ritter and Marcus confirm in almost perfect unison.

"He died!"

"Nah, he's just taking a break, like the King," Marcus says.

"Elvis or the Goblin King?" Cindy asks.

"Both," the brothers repeat.

"Goblin celebs do that after forty or so years," Marcus explains. "Before people start asking why a dude or chick in their sixties still looks thirty."

"So he's . . . what . . . like, their general?"

"And a legend," Ritter says. "The greatest goblin warrior in ten thousand years, they say."

Cindy is livid. "How do you not tell me the baddest musical virtuoso of my lifetime is, one, alive, and two, some kind of unmatched goblin general ten-thousand-year warrior legend–type motherfucker?"

"We've been busy," Ritter reminds her.

Marcus, on the other hand, is practically giddy. "All I know is if what they whisper about him is true, every green asshole down there is about to find out what it sounds like when doves cry."

The primeval sounding horn winds once more, and both battalions of the Royal Goblin Army charge in perfect collaboration, converging on the footed Vig'nerash from both sides. The demons gnash their teeth and raise their artisan blades, meeting the attack with the violent glee one would expect from minions of Hell, but it belies how immediately overmatched their forces are by the stampede of heavy horses and the trained blades being wielded from their backs. Though the Vig'nerash warriors at the forefront do manage to take the leg of the odd mount, most of them are brutally trampled under hoof before a goblin sword has the chance to reach them. The demons who feel the wrath of those blades are the warriors three rows into the Vig'nerash formation. Their pole axes are batted aside with finesse before their plastic armor and Armani bodysuit–covered shoulders are split from their scaly chests.

"Look at their swords!" Cindy cries with a manic amazement. "Look at 'em!"

Lena has to squint to zero in on what Cindy is talking about, but she sees it. The hilts of almost every goblin sword seem to be fashioned from entertainment-award statues or statuettes. The Emmys are the easiest to spot because of their bulbous skeletal "atom" sculptures and the wings of the golden woman holding them, but Lena is certain she spies Oscars, Grammys, Tonys, People's Choices, and even the odd Cable Ace Award, which she's pretty sure is a thing that doesn't even exist anymore.

The Goblin General in Purple steers his mount through the sea of bodies so effortlessly, it's as if his horse is sailing, or as if the animal has the grace and fluidity of the man astride it. He swings his sword arm in broad arcs, swiping on one side of his mount then the other. Demon heads are lopped off with the ease and rhythm of a dance, and each time he strikes, the general lets loose a melodic battle cry that rises to the rooftop, lyrical and with perfect pitch but also something guttural and vaguely sexual in tone and delivery.

"This is the greatest thing I've ever seen in my whole life," Cindy marvels, watching him. "Like, even better than seeing him play live. Which I never did. But I heard it was lit as fuck."

Marcus suddenly leaps up onto the tips of his steel-toed boots, waving his arms in excitement as if he's at a sporting event and just witnessed an impossible scoring play. "Dude, did you see that? The guy who plays Aquaman just threw his axe so hard, it went *through* one demon and into the demon *behind him*!"

"I hear they call him 'The Conqueror,'" Ritter offers matter-of-factly.

"He can conquer my panties anytime," Cindy mutters.

Marcus looks over at her, his enthusiasm vanishing, replaced by the hurt-feelings look of a very small child.

"Boy, get over yourself," Cindy chastises him. "I mean, you're cute, but *damn*."

Their voices begin to fade far away for Lena. It's all too surreal. Moments ago, she was coming to terms with the fact they were all most certainly going to be killed, and this after mourning the brutal loss of her mentor, and now they're watching everyone who has been interviewed on the E! Channel in the last five years slaughter a demon horde in the middle of Long Island City.

Even for an employee of Sin du Jour, there's only so much a person can take.

The Royal Goblin Army overcomes the majority of the Vig'nerash clan's force in a matter of minutes. With their ranks collapsed, the demons begin fleeing in any direction not barred by the path of an armored horse and a sword-wielding member of the Hollywood elite. A few even try to escape through the devastated front entrance of Sin du Jour itself, but they're cut down by the halberds of a bubbly YouTuber who does makeup tutorials and a blonde woman who makes videos about living with ADHD.

The clamor of battle begins to die down as the stallions clop carefully over the forms of slain demons littering the street. There's the odd reptilian hissing as a soldier delivers a mercy blow to a mortally wounded Vig'nerash warrior, or a stray whinny, but they are only spikes in otherwise eerie silence that settles over the scene.

The General in Purple's mount glides from the center of the battlefield and leaps onto the sidewalk in front of what used to be Sin du Jour's front doors. He idles there, turning his piercing gaze to the ledge of the roof and the half-dozen of them lined up there. His smile flashes under the pale light of the moon with the heavenly fire of comets breaking apart in the atmosphere, and he raises his Love Symbol–hilted sword in salute to them all.

"Never stop living in your hearts, Sin du Jour!" he calls to them in his unmistakable and singular voice. "It's the home we all share!"

None of them knows what to say to that. Fortunately, the slight general doesn't wait for a response before galloping off to muster his fellow goblin troops.

When Cindy finally breaks the silence, she sounds as if she's about to cry. "Y'all, I want the last ten seconds to keep happening forever."

"I'm just glad we get ten more seconds," Lena says, her eyes finding Ritter's once more, only now the look they exchange is open to the future instead of resigned to fate.

"It's never enough," he says quietly.

Darren's voice rips them both from the moment. "Sometimes, it's too much."

Lena looks back at him, seeing the ghosts that still haunt the space behind his eyes and probably always will. Her heart suddenly feels as though it's being twisted inside her chest.

"We're still here," she assures him. Then, forcing as much levity into her tone as she can muster, "And, dude, you apparently still have superhuman evil Darren strength. So, you got *that* going for you."

His expression doesn't change at first. Darren still looks as though he's just attended his own funeral.

Then, just barely yet clearly enough to lift Lena's entire being in that moment, he grins.

She smiles back at him, gratefully, feeling new tears well up in her eyes.

Marcus is completely oblivious to these subtle emotional exchanges, his attention still utterly focused on the bizarre field of battle below.

"I think I just saw Oprah take a demon's eyes as her trophies," he says. "Actually, nah, never mind. Couldn't have been."

# THE DEBT

"We should get downstairs," Ritter says to the rest of them gathered on the rooftop. "We still need to check on—"

It's as though his voice is violently sucked down into his chest. Ritter's right hand flies to his chest, fingertips digging through his shirt.

"Ritt?" Cindy asks, concern washing over her as she reaches for his other arm. "Ritt, what the hell?"

Ritter drops to his knees, still clutching his chest. The others quickly encircle him, wanting to come to his aid but trying not to crowd him at the same time.

"I'm okay," he assures them all in a constricted voice.

But he's not. The twisting in his chest, like an invisible blade, only churns more painfully. Ritter's distressed gaze falls between their bodies, glimpsing the rooftop door. At that moment, the confusion on his face melts away. He looks up at Cindy, then to his brother and finally Lena, his gaze settling on her.

Ritter smiles.

"I'm okay," he says, and there is a quiet and undeniable

acceptance in the words.

His hand falls from his chest. The rest of Ritter's body slumps gently to the ground.

Marcus can barely speak through staccato breaths of panicked shock. "Holy fucking Christ. Is he . . . is he . . ."

Cindy crouches low and checks Ritter's pulse, her face almost blank as she confirms, "He's gone."

"The debt is paid," a new voice informs them.

Cindy stands and the rest of them whirl around to see Cassandra standing in the light of the rooftop doorway.

Marcus stands and racks his shotgun, pointing it at her head. "You goddamn harpy *bitch*!"

"Did you do this?" Cindy demands, tears staining her cheeks as she unhooks her tomahawk and draws her dagger.

Cassandra says nothing, only stares at them coldly, hands folded in front of her.

"You start talking *now* or I'm going to cut you in fucking half!" Marcus yells at her.

"It was his choice," Cassandra calmly explains. "It was his offering. His life for our aid in this fight, and to balance the scales."

"Bullshit!" Cindy practically spits at her.

Cassandra shrugs. "Believe what you will. The bargain was struck. He offered his life to us freely. His only condition was that we leave his brother in peace. Personally, I hope you never find peace, Marcus Thane. You don't deserve peace. Neither of you do. But you will have no fear of us. I honor my commitments. As he honored his."

"I don't give a single solitary fuck what you say or what he did," Cindy says with a deadly coldness. "I'm about to split that Cousin It wig of yours in half."

She strides forward with every intention of cutting Cassandra down. The solitaire never moves, nor does her expression change. Perhaps she has a defensive spell in place, but what halts Cindy is Lena, who steps between Cassandra and the blades and shotgun threatening her.

"Stop," she orders Cindy, eyes darting to Marcus as well.

"You move," Cindy warns her quietly. "She doesn't get away with this. Uh-uh. She doesn't cut him down right in front of me and—"

"He's dead! He's dead and it was his choice and this isn't what he would want you to do and you know it, and if you're his friend, then you have to honor that, however the fuck you feel!"

Cindy shakes her head, eyes judging Lena venomously. "You cold bitch."

Lena's expression only hardens further, though new tears well quietly beneath her eyes. She looks from Cindy to Marcus.

"Do you want another woman's blood on your

hands?" she asks him. "Do you want to put that on your brother, too? Haven't you killed enough of them?"

The questions hit him like a fist. Marcus stares over the barrel of his shotgun at Cassandra, and in that moment, Lena knows he no longer sees the woman. Marcus is staring into the faces of every woman, every girl he and Ritter and their team of witch hunters murdered.

He lowers his weapon.

"She's right," he tells Cindy, hoarsely. "Fuck it, she's right."

Cindy takes a deep, angry breath. Her eyes fall harshly on Marcus, then back to Lena.

"I don't care what he did," she repeats.

"You don't have to care," Lena says. "But Ritter did care. And you have to respect that. He made his choice, and it was his to make."

Cindy slowly nods. She lowers the tomahawk and carefully sheathes her dagger.

"Don't ever let me see you again, bitch," she says to Cassandra. "Don't let me see you or any of your vanilla sisters, not ever. Because I will rain the fire of God himself down on y'all if I do, and you better believe that."

Cassandra nods her head just once. Stepping back through the access door, she turns and disappears down the stairwell.

Cindy walks back to where Ritter is curled upon the

rooftop. She drops her tomahawk, kneeling beside his shoulders. As she strokes his cheek with her fingertips, her tears come on in earnest, torrential in their fury.

"My beautiful boy," she whispers between tidal waves. "You beautiful, stupid boy."

Lena finds she can't watch, feeling the resolve she displayed threatening to crack like ice at the edge of winter. She lowers her head and closes her eyes, fighting her own tears.

Darren walks up and slides an arm around her shoulders. She lets her temple rest against his.

Marcus refuses to cry, but the pain is etched on his face all the same.

"Was all this shit worth it?" he asks Lena. "Was it really? Just to cook some food?"

"It's not about food," Lena says. "It's about family. You'll understand that if you stick around long enough."

For a moment, it seems as if Marcus will meet that sentiment with his trademark cynicism, but somehow, he's run out of words; they all have.

All they can do is stand there among the fallen, atop the roof of the only real home most of them have ever known, hoping the fight has finally, gratefully passed.

# PART III

# WAR IN THREE COURSES: CLEARING THE TABLE

# RED TAPE

"You again," the little nebbish clerk greets Bronko with an utter lack of enthusiasm.

Bronko sighs. "Me again, yeah."

The television studio around them is dark. The bandstand is empty. The set of Bronko's late-nineties cable cooking show has been broken down. He's been sitting on an apple crate for what feels like five minutes and a hundred years at the same time. The last time Bronko laid eyes on this place, he was made to butcher an exact replica of himself over and over again before a live studio audience of animated mannequins. He was freed from that torment only because he'd sold his soul to Allensworth before becoming Sin du Jour's executive chef. With their contract torn to pieces, Bronko had no illusions about walking out of this place a second time.

Yet here he is, and the torment hasn't picked back up.

Bronko recognizes the "man" who sprang him from the personalized torture scene before, and who is now standing in front of him again. The small, balding underworld clerk wears the same gray suit and red vest, the same wire-rimmed spectacles, and carries the same clipboard and old-style lead pencil sharpened to just shy of a nub.

He also looks terribly annoyed with Bronko.

"Mr. Luck—"

"*Chef* Luck, if you please, sir."

"Chef Luck, do you have any idea how many people die on Earth every day?"

"I don't think *a lot* would be an incorrect answer."

"And of the people who die on Earth every single day, do you know how many are remanded to what you in the English-speaking Western Hemisphere holding Christian derivative values and/or mythology refer to as *hell*?"

"Again, I imagine it's a lot."

"And of the people who die on Earth every single day who are then remanded to our custody, do you have any notion how many of *those* cases I personally handle?"

Bronko says nothing.

"*All* of them," the clipboard-toting hellion informs him.

"I see."

"Why is it, then, statistically speaking, I seem destined to deal with this one case throughout eternity? And by *this case,* I obviously mean *you.*"

"I honestly haven't a clue, fella."

The clerk licks the tip of his impossibly worn-down pencil and consults his clipboard with a sigh.

"You are not supposed to be here," he says.

"Yes, I am," Bronko contradicts him.

"No, you are not," the clerk insists, his impatience growing.

"Allensworth ripped up my contract."

"Yes, yes, I have the third-party transfer form right here. I shouldn't, however, because it should've been sent to the correct department. I reiterate, you are not supposed to be here."

"But I . . . My life . . . The things I did . . . The way I was . . ."

"Yes, according to my records, you were slated for remand here until your fortieth year on Earth. Before that time, you lived a selfish life filled with the betrayal and neglect of friends, family, and loved ones. You were spiteful, even vengeful, not to mention greedy. Oh, you'll be happy to know the man you hit with your car in Saginaw, Michigan, in 1997 before fleeing the scene lived. He subsequently forgave the driver, you, and apparently found God or Buddha or Yahweh or whatever the trendy name is on Earth for that over-publicized human resources manager now."

"Wait, wait, wait! Are you tellin' me . . . are you sayin' . . . I redeemed myself, somehow?"

"I wouldn't put it that grandiosely, but the result is the same, yes."

"That's . . . that's impossible. I didn't . . . I didn't *do* anything. I didn't have the chance to . . . That bastard Allensworth just up and did me—"

"Yes, *he*, on the other hand, is here and will be for a very, very long time. I don't envy his stay, either. Apparently, he sponsored an ill-fated coup against the boss. He and the elders of the Vig'nerash will *not* be receiving such a reprieve, I assure you."

"I mean, that's swell and all, but my point is I never had the chance to do anything—"

"What? Sacrificial? Saintly? Epic? You people, you humans, you think in such self-serving terms. This idea of the ultimate act of redemption . . . I don't carry a giant set of scales, Chef Luck; I carry a ledger. You have columns. You filled up one column with indefensible acts, and then you filled up a slightly longer column with selfless ones. You spent every day of the latter portion of your earthly existence helping, guiding, and teaching others. It's a simple concept, Chef Luck, of checks and balances. I could show you a graph if it would help."

"It's just . . . it's hard to believe—"

"Yes, I know. You no doubt had visions of sacrificing yourself to save another or the world or a busload of children. You all harbor those fantasies. There is no one big redemptive act, Chef Luck."

"There isn't?"

"No. It's never about giving your life. It's about *living* your life. And you lived enough of yours well enough to make the difference. That's all."

"So . . . I mean . . . does that mean I get to y'know, go back? Like last time?"

The clerk laughs. "No, sir, no. You *died*. You are dead. Without your soul contractually bound to an earthly holding entity, it was permanently separated from your body, which is now decomposing at the standard rate."

"Then what's going to happen to me?" Bronko asks. "Where will I go?"

The little man shrugs. "I'm afraid I don't have a form here for that," he says.

# GRAND REOPENING

"I swear, I have rebuilt and redesigned this lobby more times than I've done anything else in my career!"

Jett carefully unpeels the paint and drywall dust–spattered clear plastic coveralls protecting her Chanel sweat suit. Balling up the coveralls, she tosses them in a nearby construction debris bin. Planting her fists on her hips, she stands back to admire the newly painted drywall. She's chosen a vibrant yellow, and you'd never know a horde of meat-puppet copies of the current President of the United States piloted by fanatically patriotic gremlins had crashed through the doors and windows.

"You done good, Jett," Lena praises her. "You're the one who really holds this place together. Literally, I mean."

Jett almost blushes. "Why, thank you, Executive Chef Tarr."

Nikki, leaning against the reception desk beside Lena, begins giggling madly.

Lena reddens. "Thank you. Thank you both. You're really helping me ease into this massive transition gradually."

"Sorry," Nikki says. "I just know how much a part of you hates hearing that."

Jett waves her hand dismissively. "You'll get used to it. You're going to be a fantastic boss. I have an eye for administrative talent."

Lena isn't so sure, but accepting the responsibility was her only choice. The morning after the battle at Sin du Jour between Allensworth's forces and the staff that claimed far too many people close to Lena, a small army of unmarked cargo trucks surrounded the war-torn building. They all thought they were screwed until a tall man with beautifully sculpted blond hair and wearing a suit worth more than Lena's first two cars disembarked one of the cabs.

"Good morning," he'd greeted the confused survivors. "My name is Allensworth."

"Of course it is," Lena had said. "Why the fuck wouldn't it be?"

Their third consecutive Allensworth was entirely unruffled by and understanding of the reception. He explained that the coup staged by his predecessor's predecessor had failed, thanks in large part to Sin du Jour. If Allensworth had forgone his petty vengeance on the catering company in favor of solidifying his new regime, what was left of the Sceadu might not have had time to regroup. As things stood, that move by Allensworth compromised all the ground he'd gained with his murderous power play on Consoné and Allensworth's replacement.

Not to mention Darren killing Allensworth and the rest of the staff devastating his private army saved the Sceadu a lot of trouble.

While there were still a great number of issues to sort out, the newest Allensworth offered to renew Sin du Jour's contract, but only if Lena agreed to take over for Bronko as executive chef and run it for him.

It was the first time she'd legitimately been given a choice about working at Sin du Jour, and Lena found it was now no choice at all.

She accepted.

Allensworth III and his people cleaned up the aftermath of the battle. Lena negotiated reparations for the gnomes who had come to their aid, and amnesty for Cassandra and all of the solitaires, who would no longer be hunted. Lena found she couldn't hate Cassandra, just as she couldn't truly forgive Ritter for what he'd done in his past.

---

They haven't yet held a memorial service for Bronko, Dorsky, Ryland, White Horse, and Ritter.

They will, but even with Sin du Jour restored and repaired, it still feels too soon.

"It all looks really good, Jett," Nikki confirms. "It feels . . . new. Clean. But still us. You know?"

Lena nods, knowing exactly what she means.

There's a faint scratching at the outside of the locked lobby doors. As they all turn their heads toward it, the scratching becomes louder and more insistent.

"What the hell now?" Lena says with an exasperated sigh.

"Think positive!" Nikki bids her.

"Uh-huh."

Lena unlatches the doors and pulls them open. When she steps aside, a gobsmacked look on her face, a small, slightly unkempt Maltese trots his way inside the lobby.

"Oh, my God," Jett gasps.

"It *is*!" Nikki confirms excitedly. "It's him! He's back!"

She immediately drops to her knees and claps her hands. The Maltese sprints over to her and rears back on his tiny hind legs to lick her face. Giggling, Nikki begins stroking and tickling the small dog to his ultimate delight.

"Who's a good little creator of all things?" she playfully chides the small dog as he rolls over onto his back so Nikki can scratch his belly. "Who's an adorable most powerful being in the universe? Is that you? Is it?"

"Nik, stop!" Lena chastises her. "It's . . . He's not a . . .

You know what he is! Knock it off!"

"But he's *so* cute!" she protests.

"What's ... um ..." Jett lowers her voice, although why isn't clear. "What's *He* doing here?"

As if in answer to her question, the Maltese rights himself, standing on all four legs and barking at the open door.

They all follow the puppy's gaze expectantly. A moment later, a large American bulldog saunters into the lobby. He must be upward of a hundred pounds, his coat soft white with islands of rich brown. He's wearing a spiked collar with a shining tag that's partially obscured by his heavy, wrinkled jowls.

"Oh, he has a friend!" Nikki proclaims, crawling across the lobby floor without hesitation to pet the bulldog.

"So, who's this one? Saint Peter?" Lena asks.

"Lena!" Jett hisses. "Don't be so disrespectful!"

Nikki ignores them both, preoccupied with two handfuls of jowls. "Oh, you're a good boy, aren't you? And look at these crinkle chubs! These are *free*! They come *with*! Free crinkle chubs are the best!"

The bulldog responds to the languid massaging by gratefully licking Nikki's face, only eliciting more giggles from the pastry chef.

Her giggling abruptly stops as her fingers seize upon his nametag and she actually looks at it.

"What is it?" Lena asks, watching Nikki's expression change.

"Lena... come here."

Lena walks over to where Nikki is still cradling the bulldog, kneeling down beside them.

"Look," Nikki instructs her, turning the collar's tag so Lena can read its face.

"'Lucky,'" Lena all but whispers, narrating the single word etched on the tag.

"You don't think..." Nikki can't even finish the thought.

Lena shakes her head. "No. There's no way. It's impossible."

However, as the bulldog turns his head to regard Lena with a pair of deep, soulful eyes, she finds her lip quivering and tears threatening to well up.

"It can't..." Lena's voice goes hoarse for a moment, and she loses the words.

She clears her throat. Then: "Chef?"

The bulldog barks, just once.

Jett's hands fly to her mouth. "It's Byron!"

Lena sniffs, her eyes wet now. She reaches up and gently strokes the dog's ears.

"Chef, is it really you?"

Again, the bulldog barks.

Lena's eyes widen. In the next moment, she's throwing

her arms around the dog's neck before she can stop herself and hugging him close. Inside her, the finely honed cynic she's cultivated can no longer be heard. There's too much of her that not only wants this but also needs it.

The American bulldog that is apparently the reincarnation of Bronko Luck licks her neck.

Lena turns her head, still holding him, and looks at the Maltese, who is watching the scene unfold on his tiny haunches.

"Thank you," she whispers.

Lena and Nikki continue stroking Lucky's coat, Jett shuffling over to join them.

"Not a bad way to spend your retirement, I guess, Chef," Lena says to the dog, who responds with another enthusiastic bark.

After a time, the Maltese trots over and gently scratches at Nikki's ankle.

"What is it, little guy?" she asks happily, and then it dawns on her. "Oh! I know!"

Nikki stands and quickly jogs from the lobby. Lena and Jett exchanged confused glances, waiting in silence until Nikki returns, still jogging, carrying a frozen cupcake in each hand. Their rich green tops mark them as her trademark spumoni cupcakes composed of cherry-filled chocolate and pistachio frosting.

Nikki places them both on the ground, and the Maltese quickly sets to thawing the cold frosting with his tongue. Lucky also breaks away from Lena to chomp the lump of frosting from the top of the other cupcake.

Lena stands, Nikki joining her and Jett in watching the dogs, both of whom are far more than they seem, enjoy the treats.

Lena looks at Nikki and smiles.

"Wonders," she says.

That one word brings a look of pure joy to Nikki's face. She nods. "I knew you'd come around. Eventually."

# I WILL ALWAYS BE HERE

Lena smells the candles burning from the corridor outside before she even enters Boosha's apothecary.

There are five of them lining the top of the lectern, white beeswax touched by the softest yellow, like the very beginning of decay. An inch of gentle flame dances around each wick.

"What are the candles for?" Lena asks, the lack of greeting as customary and honored between them as any obligatory greeting could ever be.

"Who," Boosha corrects her without looking up from the near-fossilized book splayed atop the lectern.

Lena nods. "I figured. That's very uh . . . Catholic of you. I didn't think you were religious. At least, not regular-type people religion."

Boosha regards her over the book and between the wax bars of the candles.

"What is 'regular people'?"

"There aren't any, I guess. Sorry."

"Must keep candles burning until witching hour," Boosha explains, "when souls of fallen leave this place. Is old kobold custom. I have little kobold in me."

"I don't even know what that is."

"You will learn. You are boss now. Boss must know these things."

"Will you ever be done teaching me?"

Boosha nods. "One day. And then I light candle for you."

Tremors begin to wrack Lena's composure. The hard tears of grief feel like sudden bricks beneath her eyes. She has to shut her eyelids tight to contain them.

"Is okay to cry for them," Boosha gently assures her.

Lena shakes her head, sucking air through her nostrils. "It's not even for them. It's for me. Every time I think about having to keep doing this without them—"

"Is also okay to cry for you," Boosha insists. "Does not make you weak or selfish. Makes you regular people."

The ancient woman offers Lena a grin, and despite everything, Lena finds herself grinning back.

"At least I still have you," she says.

"Have much more than me," Boosha points out. "Have everything you need. Have *who* you need."

"I know." Lena wipes her damp eyes with the sleeve of her smock. "But they're looking to me to lead them now, like Chef, and I'm not him. I'm not even close."

"Do not need to be Bronko. You must be you. Is only way."

Lena laughs wryly. "Yeah, right, but is it enough?"

Boosha shrugs, returning her eyes to the runic lines in her book.

"Is what you make it," she offers.

Lena nods, gazing aimlessly at the array of junk filling the old woman's cramped quarters. There are shelves crammed with nothing but pots of various shapes, sizes, and materials, many of which probably fed people during the Great Depression, if not the Dark Ages.

It's oddly comforting, Lena finds, all of this stuff finding its way through such a long and bloody history to surround them now. Much like Boosha, it's a constant, reminding Lena that even after the traumatic events of the past few days, she's still here.

"Did you know?" she asks Boosha. "Did you know how it would work out? I mean, really? Did you know?"

"Knew only what I told you," Boosha assures her. "Knew some things would end while others carry on. Like always."

"You also said you saw me standing."

"Yes."

"Did you mean after . . . Did you see me standing after the fight was over? Or did you mean here, now?"

Boosha looks up at her with an odd expression on her already-odd face.

"What is difference?" she asks, earnestly.

Lena sighs. "I just want to know I'm going to make it, I guess. I want to know we'll make it."

"You should go home," Boosha urges her.

"No. No, I'm going to be in my *new* office for a while," Lena says with an edge of bitterness.

Boosha smiles. "Is what I meant."

Lena tries to smile, but it fades as quickly as it appears. She's like the wall of a dam, smooth and calm on one side while inconceivable weight endlessly pressures the other, and she can't seem to control which side she feels from one moment to the next.

"Yeah," she says. "Anyway."

Lena turns toward the door, taking one step, lingering.

"I'll see you tomorrow, okay?"

"Will always be here," Boosha mutters, preoccupied as if Lena has already gone.

This time, Lena's smile is wider and lasts a few seconds longer.

*It's not so much*, Lena thinks when she becomes aware of the vanishing expression, *but it's better than yesterday.*

# OFFICE HOURS

It still doesn't feel like her office, and perhaps it never will.

Lena sits behind Bronko's desk, fingering a tear in the absolutely ancient blotter. Lucky is sprawled on the leather sofa, happily dozing. She looks over at him and wonders how much awareness he really has, questioning whether his canine brain holds or is able to recall all Bronko's human memories. She imagines it would be a blessing in a way if he can exist free of all that, living out the breed's relatively short life enveloped in the moment-to-moment joys of being a dog.

Jett told her she should redecorate the office to suit her own tastes, but Lena can't imagine changing anything. It would be like redecorating a church. Lena moves her gaze over Bronko's endless clutter and memorabilia, all the football trophies and battered gear. Her eyes linger on his beloved, and now that she considers it, kind of racist sign reading, WE DON'T SERVE WEREWOLVES. ALSO, WE DON'T SERVE WEREWOLVES.

The one addition she has made to the office's décor

is a framed photograph on the desk. It's a selfie Pacific snapped with his phone at the staff's last family meal before the battle. It's the only picture Lena's aware of that features all of them together (minus, of course, Boosha, which actually feels appropriate in a way). It hurts immensely every time she looks at the photograph, but it's the kind of pain that burns away to expose a core of warmth and joy. She plans to look at it every day until that latter sting is barely a pinprick.

Nikki, Cindy, and Little Dove enter one at a time through the open door.

"Look at you," Cindy says. "All official an' shit."

Lena manages a fairly convincing smile. Things have been polite but tentative between the two of them since the rooftop, but Lena is holding out hope time will fill that gap with something better.

"Sit down, will you?" she bids them.

Cindy and Little Dove take the chairs on the other side of the desk, while Nikki chooses to drop onto the sofa beside Lucky so she can continue to never get her fill of the bulldog's crinkle chubs.

"I'm not Bronko," Lena begins. "I really *don't* want to make a speech. Shit has happened. Bad shit. Nothing I say will fix it. But we have to get back to business while we wait for all of that not to suck quite so apocalyptically. Agreed?"

No one disagrees, at least.

"Cindy, I want you to take over Stocking & Receiving. You have seniority."

Cindy only nods. She seems neither surprised nor particularly moved by the request.

"You can keep Marcus on if you want, and hire whoever you need to replace . . . to fill the holes in the team."

"The boy'll do for now," she says, referring to Marcus.

Lena nods. "Lill, I—"

"Little Dove," she says. "If that's cool. 'Lill' was me trying to be somebody else. I know who I am now."

"Good for you," Lena says, sounding more envious than anything. "I'd really like you to take over for your grandfather, if you feel you're ready."

Little Dove smiles. "Thanks, but . . . I'm going to go back to the res. There's a lot I can do there with what I've learned. I think that's what Pop would've wanted. And it's what I want."

"I kind of thought you'd say that, actually. I had to try."

"It means a lot to me that you asked," Little Dove says. "Seriously. You've all been . . . You helped me as much as Pop did, more in a lot of ways. I'll never forget any of you."

"Likewise, hon," Nikki assures her from the couch. "You'll be the best medicine woman *ever*."

Little Dove drops her head, more than a little embarrassed. "Thanks, Nikki. I'll keep baking. I promise."

"You better!"

"Nikki?" Lena says.

"Hm?"

"Sous chef" is all Lena says.

Nikki's eyes widen. She even releases her hold on Lucky.

"What are you talking about? I thought Darren—"

"Darren has been through . . . all the things. He needs time, and he may never be ready. And even if he didn't need time, it should be you."

"It's a good choice," Cindy says, prompting a surprised but subtly grateful look from Lena.

Nikki seems genuinely taken aback. "I mean . . . I just bake."

"You can still bake," Lena assures you. "You just get to do all the other thankless crap, too. I'll give you a raise, though. I'm allowed to do that, I'm pretty sure."

"Well, I . . . yeah, sure, Lena. Whatever you need."

A smile slowly spreads across her lips as she really processes the request and her answer, and it's a sentiment Lena is happy to return.

"All right, then," she says. "That's all I've got right now. I just wanted to sort that out before anything else happens?"

"What else is going to happen?" Cindy asks.

"I have . . . *no* fucking clue," Lena answers earnestly. "But at least we all know what our jobs are when it does. We'll go from there."

"Sounds good, boss," Cindy says, rising from her chair.

Little Dove and Nikki follow suit. Saying their good-nights, they begin filing out of the office.

"Cindy, hang back one second," Lena requests.

Though she looks surprised, even reluctant, Cindy nods, waving to the other two departing women and stepping back inside the office.

Lena waits until Little Dove and Nikki should be out of earshot before she says, "I don't want to do a whole thing with us—"

"I don't either," Cindy confirms.

"I just want to . . . I need you to know something."

Cindy folds her arms over her chest. "All right, then."

Lena seems to be at a loss, as if she hadn't planned out anything for this conversation beyond that point.

"I loved him too," she finally says.

Cindy nods, unfazed. "I know you did. I know he loved you, too. But you couldn't forgive him, could you?"

Lena's expression darkens. "No," she answers, honestly. "No, I guess I couldn't."

Cindy shrugs. "Then that's all there is to be said, right?"

Lena nods. "Yeah."

Cindy offers her a weak smile before turning to leave, closing the office door behind her.

Left alone, Lena lets her body sink into Bronko's chair, feeling impossibly small in the throne-like seat, almost like a child sitting at their father's desk. She looks once again at the framed picture of the staff, and once again, the pain in her chest is hotter than fire under a sauté pan. She lets it burn, studying every detail of every smiling face in the frame, especially those of the people they've lost.

"I'll never look away, you guys," she whispers to both the dead and the living. "I promise. I'm here."

Lucky raises his head from the sofa to regard her, and Lena looks back at him, smiling despite the tears shining in her eyes.

"I'm here, Chef," she says.

The ancient-looking landline phone on the desk rings, and after several of those rings, it occurs to Lena she ought to answer the call because that's what the boss would do, and that's what she is now.

"Sin du Jour," she says into the receiver after liberating it from the cradle and pressing the handset to her ear. "This is Lena Tarr . . . Yes, I'm the executive chef . . . No, I—"

Lena furrows her brow as the voice on the other end speaks, her free hand reaching for a pad and pen from the desktop to make notes. She begins scribbling fiercely.

"No," she says into the phone. "No, we *don't* usually serve werewolves, for safety reasons, but I can't say I'm familiar with were-sloths... Yes, I'm sure they *are* very docile, but... Wait, I'm sorry, did you just say *ballroom dancing*?"

The conversation lasts another few minutes, Lena jotting down the particulars all the while. When she finally hangs up the phone, she sees Lucky's head raised from the couch and his deep-set eyes staring at her expectantly.

She leans back in Bronko's old chair, somehow feeling more comfortable in the expansive leather than she did only moments ago.

"Well," Lena says to the dog. "*This* is going to be a weird one."

# Acknowledgments

Well, here we are. This is the end. I want to thank all of Sin du Jour's regular diners who've chosen to return here again and again. I hope by the end of this book, you feel as though you've consumed a grand feast beyond your wildest expectations. Failing that, I just hope you were entertained for a while and that you laughed a little, and maybe even cried a little. I gave you my best and my weirdest, for whatever that's worth.

My final thank-you to my editor, Lee Harris, can't really be expressed in words upon a page. When I first pitched him the idea for this story, I never truly believed that three years and 250,000 or so words later, I'd be concluding the seventh volume of this series. The reason I've been able to do that is because of his belief in me and Sin du Jour, and his tireless championing of both. He also pushed and inspired me to make *Taste of Wrath* the epic television two-parter-style finale I've always wanted to write for a series.

That spirit of gratitude extends to the rest of the Tor.com Publishing crew. Irene Gallo, the best damn associate publisher in the biz, as well as Carl Engle-Laird,

Katharine Duckett, Mordicai Knode, Christine Foltzer, and the rest of the folks who keep the pirate ship pointed true north. I can't heap enough praise on Sin du Jour's constant cover designer, Peter Lutjen, who, alongside Irene and Christine, just kept topping themselves with each phantasmagorical cover they produced. Sin du Jour's copyeditors, Liana Krissoff and Richard Shealy, remain the stalwart and indispensable oarspeople of this journey, and their value can't be overstated. I'd also like to acknowledge all the reviewers who have supported and evangelized the series since our first book. They helped keep us afloat.

I want to thank my agent, DongWon Song of HMLA, ever my Hanzo sword. I want to thank Helljack, my webmaster and all-around cyber assassin. I want to thank my wife, Nikki. As I compose these acknowledgments, we are a week away from our wedding, and will have been married for many months by the time you read these words. However, that was my first time writing "my wife" and it felt more amazing than I ever imagined it would. I want to thank my mother, Barbara, who is a one-woman publicity department more enthusiastic and tireless than any publisher could possibly hope to employ. I also want to thank my mother-in-law, Jodie, who let Nikki and me live with her while our new home was under renovation, and in whose home I finished writing the first draft of

*Taste of Wrath*. This final Sin du Jour book is dedicated to her husband, my father-in-law Mitch, who left us far too soon.

Finally, and once again, thank *you*. There are no books without readers, and you helped me tell one of the best stories I've ever told. I won't forget any of you.

# About the Author

Photograph by Earl Newton

**MATT WALLACE** is the author of the Sin du Jour Affairs, *The Next Fix*, *The Failed Cities*, and the novella series Slingers. He's also penned more than one hundred short stories, some of which have won awards and been nominated for others, in addition to writing for film and television. In his youth, he traveled the world as a professional wrestler and unarmed combat and self-defense instructor before retiring to write full-time. He now resides in Los Angeles with the love of his life and inspiration for Sin du Jour's resident pastry chef.

# TOR·COM

**Science fiction. Fantasy. The universe.**

**And related subjects.**

*

More than just a publisher's website, *Tor.com*

is a venue for **original fiction, comics,** and

**discussion** of the entire field of SF and fantasy,

in all media and from all sources. Visit our site

today — and join the conversation yourself.